W9-BYQ-117

WOLFCRY

Also by Amelia Atwater-Rhodes

WOLFCRY

Amelia Atwater-Rhodes

Delacorte Press

Published by Delacorte Press
an imprint of Random House Children's Books
a division of Random House, Inc.
New York

Delacorte Press and colophon are registered trademarks of Random House, Inc.

www.randomhouse.com/teens

Educators and librarians, for a variety of teaching tools, visit us at
www.randomhouse.com/teachers

Library of Congress Cataloging-in-Publication Data
Atwater-Rhodes, Amelia.
Wolfcry / Amelia Atwater-Rhodes. — 1st. ed.
p. cm. — (The Kiesha'ra ; v. 4)
Summary: Knowing that she must soon choose a mate, twenty-year-old Oliza,
heir to the Wyvern throne that unites the avian and serpiente peoples, weighs
the political ramifications of her choice while also longing to follow her heart.
ISBN-13: 978-0-385-73195-9 (trade hardcover) — ISBN-13: 978-0-385-90354-7 (glb)
ISBN-10: 0-385-73195-7 (trade hardcover) — ISBN-10: 0-385-90354-5 (glb)
[1. Kings, queens, rulers, etc.—Fiction. 2. Birds—Fiction. 3. Snakes—Fiction.
4. Magic—Fiction. 5. Wolves—Fiction. 6. Fantasy.]
I. Title. II. Series: Atwater-Rhodes, Ameila. Kiesha'ra ; v. 4.
PZ7.A8925Wol 2006
[Fic]—dc22   2005034961

The text of this book is set in 12-point Loire.

Printed in the United States of America

10 9 8 7 6 5 4 3 2 1

First Edition

Wolfcry
is dedicated to Bethany "Fenris" Hopkins,
for inspiring me to write about wolves.

tair'feng'ha'nas
Mehay'hena-ke-tair'feng'la'Fenris
ke-o'tair'feng'ha'a'la'varl'kayla

Also,
I give thanks to:
Mike Justiana, whose gift of music came at just the right time;
Ollie, as always, for many long hours of listening and support;
Kel, for her confidence, when my own took a vacation;
Jesse, for getting me away from my books for a while;
and the tireless people at MassEquality,
for giving me faith to continue.

ke'ke
la-varl'teska-a
de'rait'varl'Kain'hena'la'Mike
a'he'ke'ke'heah-azne'nan'rai'la'Ollie
a'fide-la'vehlar'la'Kel
a'rahvis'o'la'sheni'la'Jesse
ke'ka
a'la'varl'fide
maen'MassEquality-rait'rai'ka'heah'Ahnmik

And finally,
thanks to the loyal readers at the Den, most especially:
Jordan Reed; Seán Nikolas; Rian Lizada;
Jessica "Arqueete"; Kaiya Rose Lee; and Feaad.

maen'ciab
teska-a
maen'larmaen-ksh'teinas'rsh
ke'ke-la'jaes'norvio

To faith, hope and pancakes.
a'fide-a'keyi-a'estobien'pt

a'le-Ahnleh

THE SHAPE

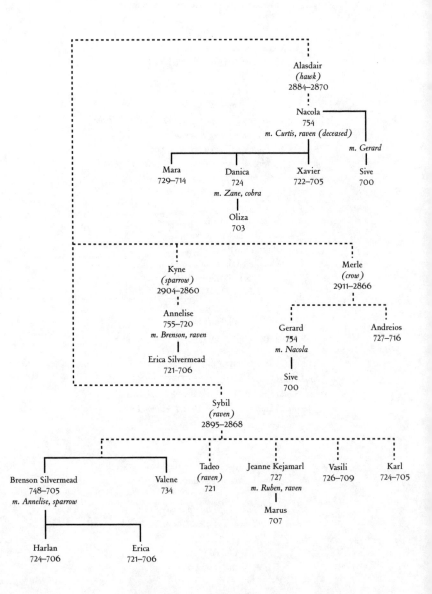

Alasdair
(hawk)
2884–2870

Nacola
754
m. Curtis, raven (deceased)
m. Gerard

Mara
729–714

Danica
724
m. Zane, cobra

Xavier
722–705

Sive
700

Oliza
703

Kyne
(sparrow)
2904–2860

Merle
(crow)
2911–2866

Annelise
755–720
m. Brenson, raven

Gerard
754
m. Nacola

Andreios
727–716

Erica Silvermead
721-706

Sive
700

Sybil
(raven)
2895–2868

Brenson Silvermead
748–705
m. Annelise, sparrow

Valene
734

Tadeo
(raven)
721

Jeanne Kejamarl
727
m. Ruben, raven

Vasili
726–709

Karl
724–705

Marus
707

Harlan
724–706

Erica
721–706

Dashed lines indicate not only a lapse of several generations, but also an indirect relation.

SHIFTERS

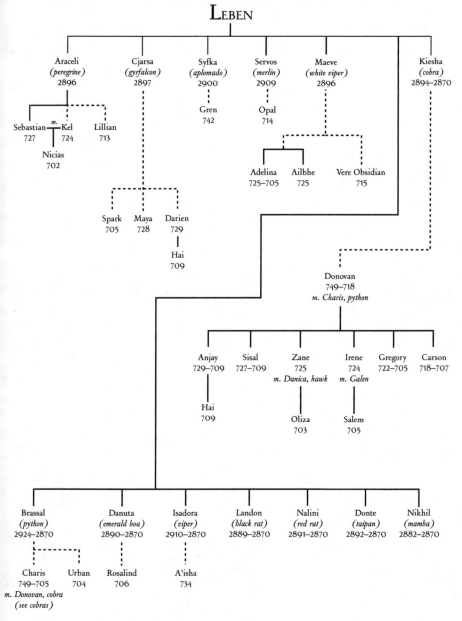

Leben

Araceli
(peregrine)
2896

Cjarsa
(gyrfalcon)
2897

Syfka
(aplomado)
2900

Servos
(merlin)
2909

Maeve
(white viper)
2896

Kiesha
(cobra)
2894–2870

Sebastian
727

m.

Kel
724

Lillian
713

Gren
742

Opal
714

Nicias
702

Adelina
725–705

Ailbhe
725

Vere Obsidian
715

Spark
705

Maya
728

Darien
729

Hai
709

Donovan
749–718
m. Charis, python

Anjay
729–709

Sisal
727–709

Zane
725
m. Danica, hawk

Irene
724
m. Galen

Gregory
722–705

Carson
718–707

Hai
709

Oliza
703

Salem
705

Brassal
(python)
2924–2870

Danuta
(emerald boa)
2890–2870

Isadora
(viper)
2910–2870

Landon
(black rat)
2889–2870

Nalini
(red rat)
2891–2870

Donte
(taipan)
2892–2870

Nikhil
(mamba)
2882–2870

Charis
749–705
*m. Donovan, cobra
(see cobras)*

Urban
704

Rosalind
706

A'isha
734

PROLOGUE

*A*nother day, and Wyvern's Court still survives. Sometimes I
fear that we are held together by nothing but hope and desperation, but those bonds have held us for a score of years.

Tomorrow is the holiday that my mother's people call Festival.
It is a day of storytelling, laughter and song for the avians. Already
the northern hills of Wyvern's Court are bright with decorations.

Meanwhile, my father's people, in the southern hills, prepare to
celebrate a serpiente event. My cousin, Salem Cobriana, will take
vows tomorrow to become a full member of the dancers' guild. He
will be the first cobra in more than eight hundred years to be em-
braced by that venerated group.

I speak of my mother's people and my father's. To which group
do I belong? Both–or neither?

I have four forms in addition to my human one. One is that of
a hawk as pure and golden as any avian queen who soared above
the land. Another is that of a black cobra, like every heir to the serpiente royal house. I also have a form that is a blend of all my
traits–a human body with wings the color of sunset, scales black like
night, garnet eyes, a hawk's vision and a cobra's poison.

My last form is that of a wyvern, a perfect blend of serpent and avian–a form that is of all my people and like none of them. The wyvern's cobra body is ruffled with feathers at its hood, spreading into wings that can drive me through the air faster than any hawk.

I am the princess of Wyvern's Court, the wyvern for which it was named, and my reign will mean the union of two worlds that warred for two millennia before my birth. Tomorrow, Festival, marks twenty-one years since my mother and father made what many considered a mad plan to bring peace to their people.

My parents ended the slaughter, the battles, the clash of armies and the generations of widows and orphans. They swore to end the killing, and for that I sing my thanks to the avians' gods of the sun and sky, and dance it to the serpents' goddess of freedom and passion. But hatred takes longer to die, and I fear sometimes that my parents' bloody memories blind them to the fear and anger that still stain this world. I see it all too clearly.

Their reign ended the killing. I pray for the strength I need for my reign to be the one to end the war.

Oliza Shardae Cobriana
Heir to the Tuuli Thea
Arami of the serpiente

CHAPTER 1

The northern hills of Wyvern's Court were filled with the trills of tiny bells, the lilting words of storytellers and the songs of choruses. Enraptured children sat in front of me, waiting for me to begin the story of the first avian queen. Blatantly out of place among them was a friend of mine, a serpiente dancer named Urban, who was lounging near the back, managing to look bored and nervous at the same time.

"Many, many years ago, our ancestors were a collection of small tribes, each led by a different captain and each squabbling with its neighbors over food, water and shelter. When drought caused famine, they became afraid and so were more protective of their scarce belongings.

"In the middle of the worst winter, when early snows had destroyed too many of the crops, a woman named Aleya gave birth to a daughter. She loved her child, but she knew she could never take care of her. So Aleya brought the beautiful golden girl to the mountains and left her there, praying that the wild spirits would care for her.

"The infant began to cry, and soon a pair bond of hawks

landed beside her. They cared for the child as one of their own, teaching her the language of the forest and giving her their most precious gift: the skies. They gave the girl some of their magic and taught her how to change from her human form into that of a golden hawk."

I paused there, looking into the wide eyes of my young audience. One of the children had moved closer to Urban and was trying to examine the silk scarf he had tied around his waist—a *melos,* one of the accessories worn by professional serpiente dancers. Urban glanced at her and she jumped.

"But there comes a time when every chick must leave its nest, and as she grew older, the hawk-girl began to wonder about her true mother. Finally, when she was thirteen, she returned to her homeland. She found her mother and her younger brother, whom she had never known, but was horrified by the conditions in which they lived, by the fear and anger that seemed ever present among humans.

"The girl led first her family and then the rest of her mother's tribe into the woods and taught them how to reach the skies. She showed them better ways to hunt, with a hawk's vision and talons, and so they became healthy and well fed once again.

"Later, other tribes joined them, and each took a form from the wilderness—ravens, crows and then sparrows. For the first time, these tribes lived peacefully together, led by the young queen they named Alasdair, which means *protector.*"

The children clapped happily, making the bells hanging from their wrists jingle.

I smiled, enjoying the story almost as much as I had during my first Festival—until one of the adults who had been nearby noticed her child reaching for Urban's *melos* again and darted forward to scoop her up and away from Urban. Urban pretended not to notice, but I saw his back tense.

I had told the story of Alasdair the way my mother had used to tell it to me, but I knew that some of these children had learned a darker ending from their parents. Just twenty years before, the myth always would have included the death of Alasdair at the hands of the serpiente. Tales such as these fueled avians' hatred from the cradle.

I tried not to let the avian mother's reaction to Urban ruin my mood. I knew that many people did not approve of his presence there; Urban was not just a serpent—an apprentice dancer, at that—he was widely known to be my foremost suitor among the serpiente. As such, he faced the wrath of mothers with eligible sons, and of course the jealousy of avian men our age, in addition to the general prejudice of avians against serpiente.

Still, I was glad he had come. Suitor or not, Urban was one of my closest friends. We had grown up together. It meant a lot to me that he was willing to be there even though he knew how the avians might react.

"Bit of a dull story," Urban remarked as he came to my side, trying to keep a careful distance between himself and the avians around us. "Lacks intrigue, danger, scandal."

"Well, I'm sorry that the way my ancestor saved her people from starvation and war isn't racy enough for you," I said, teasing.

Serpiente history—which, unlike the avian stories, was regarded as fact, not myth—involved the brave leader of a clan known as the Dasi seducing a powerful creature called Leben, who had impersonated one of their gods to demand their worship. The story, which was told each year in the dance named after the winter solstice holiday Namir-da, described how Leben had given all of Maeve's people second forms to try to win her favor. Maeve had been given the form of a white viper. Kiesha, the high priestess of Anhamirak, had been given the form of a king cobra. Seven others had been given serpent forms, and four, the followers of the god Ahnmik, had been given falcon forms.

The *Namir-da* did not tell the falcons' story. It also did not include the part about the Dasi being torn apart by a vicious civil war shortly after the gifts had been given. Maeve and the four falcons had been exiled on charges of black magic. The white vipers still lived on the fringes of our society even in modern day, while Cjarsa, Araceli, Syfka and Servos made up the royal house of the falcon empire. Kiesha's people became the serpiente; my family were her descendents.

"Unfortunately," Urban continued, his tone making clear that he found nothing unfortunate in it, "I need to run to the nest now. I'm hoping to catch Salem before he is surrounded by people." Only the full members of the dancer's nest had been invited to Salem's initiation ceremony, and though Urban had grown up in the nest, he had not yet taken his vows. However, the reception that night would be open to anyone who wanted to attend, including apprentices and wyverns. "You will be there later, right?"

"Of course. I think my parents have already headed over."

He looped an arm around my waist and kissed my cheek. By serpiente standards, the gesture was friendly and casual, but by avian standards, it was shockingly forward—so much so that someone immediately grabbed Urban's arm to drag him away from me.

"I'm sorry," Urban instantly said, smiling at the young

man who had come to my unnecessary but well-intentioned rescue. "Did you want a kiss, too?" Marus, the avian, blushed the color of a robin's breast, which prompted Urban to add, "Hmm. I'm sure you did—just not from me."

As Marus stammered, Urban raised his hands innocently. "Sorry, Oliza, Marus, but what can I say? I agreed to be bored to tears all day. You can't blame me for slipping up. Now I really do need to run. I'll see you later, Wyvern." He blew me a kiss on his way down the hill to the dancer's nest on the opposite side of Wyvern's Court.

"I apologize if I overreacted," Marus said to me before I could even begin to speak. "I saw him put his hands on you as I walked by, and responded without thinking."

I had known Marus for years, and while I was glad he understood that *I* would think he had overstepped his bounds, I knew he didn't really think it was inappropriate to pull an assertive suitor away from a lady.

"I appreciate your concern, but according to serpiente custom," I explained patiently, "he might as well have just smiled at me. It would have meant the same."

"According to *serpiente* custom, perhaps," Marus said, "but Urban knew where he was."

"The laws are the same on both sides of Wyvern's Court, and he hasn't broken any."

"They might be the same on both sides, but they change according to blood. Urban took advantage of the fact that you allow a serpent to behave in a manner that you would consider utterly inappropriate from an avian like me—and he did it specifically because he knew that it would offend the dozens of people who were watching."

What he said horrified me, because to a large extent it

was true. I wanted my people to be treated equally, but even I dealt with avians and serpiente quite differently, assigning to each a different set of rules.

What choice did I have? I couldn't judge my people only by avian or serpiente standards, and asking them to behave according to the customs of the area they were in meant that we might as well still have two courts. Between a culture in which it was inappropriate to display strong emotion and another in which it was rude not to, one world where touching was vulgar and another where lack of contact was an insult, there was no easy middle ground. There certainly wasn't one that wouldn't be considered offensive by *everyone*.

"The moral of this story," came a calm, diplomatic voice, "is that Urban can steal as many kisses as he likes, and regardless of his intent, she will always see his actions as one of a friend." I turned and was immediately face to face with seventeen-year-old Sive, the youngest daughter of my grandmother, Nacola, which technically made Sive my aunt, despite her being three years younger than I was.

Sive's hair was long and golden, and her eyes were the same color. She wore a softly flowing cream gown and her feet were bare aside from the fine golden anklet that chimed as she walked. She said, "Serpents may be freer with physical contact, and I'm sure that is a perfectly valid choice, but I imagine it is difficult to court a lady if there is nothing romantic and daring left to do."

Hearing sweet, docile Sive say the words *romantic and daring* almost made me laugh. Although Sive had grown up in Wyvern's Court, she had been raised with the strictest avian traditions. Right now Sive stood beside her avian alistair, Prentice—the nineteen-year-old man to whom she had been betrothed at her birth, a raven who had never done anything that was not careful and reserved.

Sive's comment pacified Marus, but it did not settle my own thoughts—partially because I continued to worry about my own prejudice, and partially because I wasn't certain I wanted Marus to take Sive's thinly veiled advice to be "romantic and daring." In avian society, a lady who accepted a kiss on the cheek from a suitor might as well have accepted a proposal. I wasn't ready to choose my king.

I could think of only one way to avoid the potential problem: give Marus something to do before he thought up something on his own.

"Unfortunately, we must continue this conversation later," I said, "since I plan to attend Salem's reception."

"I thought you said you couldn't go," Marus said.

"To the ceremony itself," I clarified. "Salem's initiation is a major event—not just for the dancers but for all serpiente, since it means the return of the royal family to the nest. The reception is open to anyone who wants to attend."

Marus's eyes did not quite glaze over, but despite his best attempt to show an appropriate level of interest, it was obvious that he cared as much about the formal ending of an eight-hundred-year-old feud between the nest and the Cobriana as Urban cared about famine among Alasdair's warring tribes.

"You're welcome to join me," I offered.

"Us," Sive corrected. "I promised Salem I would make an appearance."

"Sive . . ." Prentice's cultured tones didn't quite conceal his distress. "Didn't you decide not to attend?"

I wasn't surprised by the raven's reaction. Prentice was horrified anytime Sive chose to be around serpents.

He didn't care for me, and I didn't care for him, but he and Sive seemed to get along well enough. If the hawk resented having no choice in the matter, she did not express the sentiment aloud. Avian ladies had always had their pair bonds chosen for them by their parents. I was thankful that my parents had decided to follow serpiente tradition, allowing me to pick my own mate—though occasionally I wondered if it would have been easier if the choice had been made for me.

Sive arched one golden brow. "No," she said, "I believe I told you that *you* did not need to attend, if you are so uncomfortable around serpiente. Since Salem, Oliza and her parents, Zane and Danica, will be there, I am sure to be quite adequately chaperoned."

"Marus?" I prompted.

He started to shake his head, then paused, taking a moment to evaluate my very serious expression. "This isn't just a friendly invitation, is it?"

I shook my head and answered honestly. "Marus, you were upset that Urban kissed my cheek because you know that he is also courting me, and you fear it means that I allow him more liberties than I do you. Sive and I both told you that it meant nothing. I'll go one step further in telling you why:

"I'm not an avian lady, to be courted with poetry and flowers. I'm not a serpiente dancer, who can be impressed by a *harja* and a gift of a handmade *melos*. I am the wyvern of Wyvern's Court, and I cannot afford to choose as my king a man who is not able to accept both sides of me, and both sides of this land. If you are going to feel threatened by Urban, it shouldn't be because he kissed me. It should be because he came with me to the northern hills during Festival.

Avian merchants watched him as if certain he was going to steal from them. Alistairs and parents stepped between him and any lady or child he stood too near or—sky forbid—tried to talk to. In short, they treated him worse than they would have treated a beggar wolf from the forest. But he stayed.

"You say you are trying to court me. So, if you're going to feel challenged by anything, feel challenged by *that*."

What could he possibly say?

He drew a deep breath and then nodded. "Then . . . I accept your invitation."

CHAPTER 2

E ven for someone raised partially in the serpiente nest, as I was, there were sights capable of stopping thought and even breath. A professional dancer who takes the stage to perform a *harja* for a man she desires is one such sight.

As we moved through the crowd, Marus followed me closely and tried to stay calm. We had almost reached Salem when I saw Rosalind Lakeyi step onto the dais. If her relationship with Salem had not already been common knowledge, it would have been made clear by the lingering look she sent his way as she rose onto the balls of her feet, stretching her spine and arching her back in a pose I recognized. It was the starting position for the solo in the Namir-da dance: Maeve's seduction of Leben, one of the most famous and most complex of the *harja*.

The dance was accompanied only by a single drum, which pounded like a heartbeat, driving the pulses of the audience faster as our minds and bodies were hypnotized by each dip and turn Rosalind took. At some point I heard Sive whisper, "Oh, my," and turn away, as if her instinct was to give the dancer privacy for such a display, but my gaze was as firmly locked as that of any cobra who swayed to the rhythm of the snake charmer's dance.

When it ended, we collectively let out a breath. In such a moment, it was easy to believe that our ancestors had possessed magic powerful enough to command the gods themselves.

"If I dance for you, will you look at *me* that way?"

I jumped at Urban's voice, then blushed at both his suggestion and my reaction. "You know I wouldn't let you."

An adult dancer could perform a *harja* or a *melos* at any time, technically, but it was almost always intended for someone special, and it usually ended with the new couple seeking a private alcove, and the nest elders sighing about young love. If I danced those steps, it would be taken as a sign that I had chosen my mate, or at least that I was ready to do so.

I longed to dance as freely as Rosalind did, but while friendly kisses were nearly meaningless among the serpiente, dance never was. I could let Marus steal a dozen kisses before I could let Urban get on that dais and perform a *harja* for me—much less stand up and perform one myself.

The decision I would someday make was too crucial. I wished I could base it on the pull of my heart, but there had never really been anyone who had drawn my passion in that way—not even my two foremost suitors.

I turned my attention back to Marus, who had gone pale. My guest started to speak, thought better of it, and then abruptly turned from white to crimson.

Urban whispered to me, "I bet you his last thought was 'What would Oliza look like doing that?' "

I frowned and hushed him.

Prentice approached with Sive and, looking at Salem, asked dryly, "Is that appropriate?"

My cousin had responded to Rosalind's performance in the only way serpiente *would* consider appropriate. Their kiss had gone on long enough for one of the other dancers to spin a *melos* around both their necks. Normally I would have assumed the gesture to be idle teasing, but the black silk *melos* had been decorated with intricate stitching in gold— a color that among the serpiente represented an eternal mated tie. I wondered if I would be hearing an announcement sometime soon.

Salem must have heard Prentice's question, because he focused his garnet cobra's gaze on the avian.

I stepped between the two men, clearing the way with inane chatter. The two of them had never gotten along.

"Salem, congratulations," I said. His smile warmed and he stepped forward to hug me.

Behind me, Sive was whispering to Prentice: *"Behave."*

"I will if he does."

"Thanks," Salem replied, looking around searchingly. "I saw your parents a couple of minutes ago."

"Then Rosalind distracted you?" I asked.

"I have my priorities straight. And it looks like you've brought your own distractions. Marus, this is a surprise."

"I hope I am not intruding," Marus said.

"Do you really?" Salem asked, teasing. Without giving Marus a chance to come up with a polite reply, he shook his head. "You are of course welcome, especially since I imagine that you are my cousin's guest. I have nothing against feathers. Speaking of, my blushing aunt, I seem to recall that you promised me a dance. Prentice, mind if I borrow your lovely lady a minute?"

Prentice looked like he minded quite a bit, but when Sive shot him a pointed look, he gritted his teeth and shook his head. In the spirit of the moment, I turned to Marus and offered my hand. "Care to dance?"

"No." His response was so instinctive, so abrupt, that we both laughed. Color crept up his face. "I'm no expert on serpents, but I know that almost everyone here learned to dance while learning how to *walk*."

"Not everyone." I nodded at Salem and Sive. This was maybe the third time Salem had convinced Sive to try dancing. She was abysmally bad, but Salem led well enough that she didn't embarrass herself. Despite Salem's keeping to dances that were tame by serpiente standards, appropriate for siblings or friends who weren't intimate, Prentice watched them with a scowl.

"I don't know how to dance," Marus said.

"I'll teach you." There were plenty of fairly innocent dances that were also simple enough for Marus to learn.

He was so nervous that I almost felt sorry for him as he followed me to the edge of the plaza where serpents were dancing informally. Had I not had so much invested in that night, I might have told him he could leave.

"I can't handle watching this disaster in the making," Urban announced as he jogged to catch up with us. "Marus, relax. If I can tell you're tense by watching you *walk*, you're going to have a lot of trouble dancing."

Marus looked mildly affronted, but before he could react, a shadow brushed across the ground. I looked quickly at the sky, where a single peregrine falcon was circling.

His voice a little too hopeful, Marus asked, "Do you need to go?"

The falcon was not simply any bird, but Nicias Silvermead,

the second-in-command of the Wyverns—my honor guard on the few occasions when I needed one, as well as the rarely necessary police of Wyvern's Court. Gretchen, the commander of the Wyverns, was a serpent and had requested the evening off for Salem's reception. That left Nicias in charge, which meant that his seeking me out was for official reasons. Not a good sign.

My parents also must have seen the signal. They slipped through the crowd.

"Urban, Marus, good to see you both," my mother greeted the young men politely. "Oliza?"

"Go," Urban said. "I'll take care of Marus while you're gone."

"Excuse me?" Marus chirped in surprise.

"I spent all day at your avian Festival," Urban informed him. "You aren't getting off so easy here just because there's an emergency. Give me your hand. By the time Oliza gets back, we'll have you ready for a dance."

They looked at each other for a moment, Marus shrinking somewhat with acute discomfort, and Urban's blue eyes shining as he challenged his primary competition. I could almost hear them both thinking, *Is this really worth it?* I worried about leaving them alone together, but if Nicias was looking for me, then I had bigger problems than male egos.

"I'll be back as soon as I can," I told them.

"Do you have any idea what's going on?" I asked my parents as the three of us pushed through the crowd to clearer ground.

They both shook their heads, but the answer was not long in coming. As soon as we were outside the mass of serpents, Nicias dove to the ground, transforming from a falcon into a young man with blond hair that turned silvery blue at the front, and worried icy blue eyes.

Nicias and I had been friends since infancy. The only falcon in Wyvern's Court, he was as much an anomaly as I was as the only wyvern, and that bond had made us very close. That he was the only male my age who I knew would never try to court me also helped.

He had gracefully offered to take over for Gretchen for the evening, without speaking a word of regret about not being welcome at the reception. Salem might not have anything against feathers, but many serpents were still uncomfortable around a falcon—even one born and raised in Wyvern's Court.

"Something wrong?" my mother asked. As always, Danica Shardae seemed to embody the blending of the two courts that I often tried to mimic. Her gold hair was pinned up with combs decorated with images of the serpiente goddess Anhamirak, exposing the hawk feathers at the nape of her neck and a necklace of twisted gold, with a pendant in the form of an *Ahnleh,* an ancient serpiente symbol meaning Fate. The necklace I wore every day had a coin stamped with the same symbol; it had been a gift from the dancer's nest to my mother when they had ceremonially welcomed her into their ranks, shortly before my birth. Even though my mother was dressed like a serpiente dancer right then, she held herself with the calm poise of an avian lady while listening to Nicias's report.

"I'm not sure," Nicias said. "A pride of lions entered our land a few minutes ago. The leader says he has a message for the royal house of Wyvern's Court."

All the lions I knew of worked as mercenaries. Wyvern's Court had never needed them, though they had offered to serve both the avians and the serpiente at various times during the long years of war and had occasionally been hired.

"Are they waiting in the Rookery?" I asked.

"In the courtyard, yes."

As we started toward the eastern cliffs, my mother hesitated, glancing back at Marus and Urban. "Is it a good idea to leave them together?"

"Probably not," I admitted.

"An avian and a serpiente dancing together to impress the recipient of their mutual affection," my father mused. "It is bold, but not the most surprising thing I've ever heard of young men doing in their efforts to show off. They will probably be fine."

"Probably?" I asked. The words were not as comforting as I would have liked.

CHAPTER 3

W e entered the Rookery courtyard to find six well-armed men and women watching us with a neutral attention. Every time I had spoken to the lions, they had been the epitome of courteousness, but even so, the sight of their soldiers unnerved me.

Their leader stepped forward and bowed. "Diente and alistair Zane Cobriana; Tuuli Thea and Naga Danica Shardae; Princess Oliza Shardae Cobriana. And Arami'ka Irene Cobriana," Tavisan greeted us formally as my father's younger sister—Salem's mother—stepped into the room.

"I saw the three of you leave and came in case I was needed," Irene explained when we all looked back at her.

"That's yet to be seen," my father said. "Tavisan, I understand you have a message for us?"

"I'm here on behalf of Kalisa, the alpha of the Vahamil pack," Tavisan said. The wolves' territory brushed against the northern borders of Wyvern's Court. We had always had excellent relations with them. "My pride recently stopped in Vahamil land to trade. As you know, it is our way to ask the permission of the leader of any territory we stop in, so I requested an audience with the alpha. It was . . . not entirely what I had expected.

"Kalisa has been injured, severely. I was told that it was a hunting accident. It is possible that a successor will be chosen. Kalisa says she would like her allies to be present, so that if necessary she can introduce them to the new alpha and help ensure a continuing alliance between the Vahamil and Wyvern's Court."

I was told. Kalisa says. He was being very careful with his words.

"Why does it take six soldiers to deliver a message?" I asked.

"I have given you the message, as I was requested," he replied. "Anything else I might tell you would be speculation."

I glanced at my parents, but they both nodded for me to continue. "Is there other information you feel we should know?"

"It seems odd that the Vahamil would hire an outsider to deliver such important news. Normally my pride is asked to carry messages only across terrain that those sending them could not easily cross—which is not the case with the wolves—or in times when one does not want to place an important missive in the hands of someone of questionable loyalty. I do not know exactly how precarious Kalisa's position is, or how many wolves are currently vying for leadership, but my impression is that there are not many she can trust."

The Vahamil had flourished under Kalisa's leadership, but if she was perceived as weak, under their laws any wolf would have the right to challenge her. She might have said she was sending for the rulers of Wyvern's Court to introduce us to a potential heir, but it seemed more likely now that she had called for her allies to try to protect her own throne.

My mother must have come to the same conclusion at the same moment, because she nodded and said, "We will go tonight. Our alliance with Kalisa has always been valuable to all of our people. It is important to make sure that any potential heirs appreciate that. Oliza, would you please give our regrets to Salem and the nest for needing to leave so suddenly?"

"Of course."

"Do you need me to stay in Wyvern's Court?" Irene offered reluctantly. She and my uncle, Galen, had intended to leave for the serpiente palace immediately after Salem's reception that night. From there, they were headed east and wherever Fate took them. Their plans had been nearly half a year in the making, since Irene had announced her intent to take advantage of this era of peace by traveling the world with her mate.

My father shook his head. "Oliza will be here."

I often acted in my parents' stead when they were away. As they often reminded me, I would inherit the throne as soon as I chose my mate and was ready to claim it. In the meantime, I needed to live up to my position.

"I'll send for the members of your guard to travel with you," Nicias said to my parents. "I imagine you will want to leave immediately."

"That would be best."

"If you do not require our escort," Tavisan said, "I would like to respectfully ask your permission to remain in Wyvern's Court and visit your market tomorrow to replenish our supplies. We did not have time to trade with the Vahamil."

The lions had occasionally passed through our lands for various jobs and had never caused trouble, so I said, "As long as your stay is peaceful, you are welcome in our market."

"Thank you, milady."

* * *

Irene stayed to confirm plans with my parents, assuring me that she would return to the reception before going on her way, and I started back toward the southern hills. If the events in Wyvern's Court had been anything other than the initiation of a cobra into the dancer's nest, I would have asked to go with my parents, but I understood why my remaining there was important. The dancers were the heart of the serpiente; it was essential to make clear that Salem could join them and still be part of the royal house.

Serpiente celebrations frequently lasted until dawn, but anxiety about Kalisa had stripped me of my energy. I wondered how early I would be able to leave without causing concern.

The first person I saw was not Marus or Urban but a young woman with the black hair and garnet eyes of the serpiente royal house—a cousin I had learned of only a few months before, when Nicias had brought her back from the falcon island of Ahnmik. She seemed to be watching the dancers from the edge of the crowd.

"Good evening, Hai," I said. "It is good to see you out and about."

When she did not reply immediately, I thought she had not heard me, and I wondered whether I should speak again. Hai was the only daughter of my father's oldest brother, but she had been born and raised on Ahnmik. She could pass as Cobriana, but I knew she considered herself a falcon, like her mother.

The combination of these two heritages had nearly driven her mad. When Hai had first arrived at Wyvern's Court, she had been comatose, and most people had assumed she would never recover. Even now that she was awake, it was evident that her mind was still not completely right.

"Oliza," she said to me after a moment. "Don't patronize me."

"I didn't mean to. I simply do not see you in the market much. I'm sure Salem is pleased that you are here."

She shrugged. "I'm sure the cobra has other things on his mind . . . like flirting with a pretty hawk and waiting for her alistair to hit him."

I sighed, deciding to end the conversation while it was still sane and mostly civil. I had known Hai to break into periods of complete incoherence.

"If you'll excuse me, I need to find Marus."

She nodded and replied loftily, "You're excused."

It didn't take long to find someone who could point me toward Urban and Marus. My two well-known rival suitors' attempting to dance together was a spectacle even by serpiente standards.

Aside from his jumping whenever Urban moved closer and they accidentally touched, Marus seemed to be dealing well with Urban's instruction. Every now and then one of the young men would murmur something, usually too soft for me to hear but clearly less than flattering.

Watching them gave me some hope. Neither looked exactly *happy*, but I would have been shocked if they had. After all, they were not just from opposite sides of the court, they were rivals. However, the competition seemed to have driven both of them to do something they otherwise would not have considered; Urban had issued this challenge, and Marus had accepted it.

Urban noticed my presence. He smiled at me and then moved a little closer to Marus to say something that made the raven blush. A moment later, the sound of a familiar, bell-like laugh drew my attention to where Sive and Salem were still dancing together. Prentice looked as if he was on the verge of reclaiming his pair bond, but Rosalind was doing her best to keep him occupied.

I looked away from Urban and Marus only for an instant, and in the next moment, I heard a sound that could only have been a punch connecting with skin.

I spun around just in time to see Urban stumble back, one hand going to his bleeding lip. Serpiente tempers being what they were, I had time to take exactly one step forward before Urban retaliated with a blow that sent Marus to the ground.

"I forgot. You're a bird," Urban spat. "You wouldn't recognize a come-on if it bit you."

"And you wouldn't recognize a *lady* if she slapped you," Marus retorted as he pushed himself up.

"Sure I would—one just did."

Marus made another move toward Urban, but Salem grabbed the raven's arm. That prompted Prentice to come to Marus's defense, and practically the entire population of the southern hills to come to Salem's.

Recognizing the possibility for real violence, I took a deep breath and let out a wyvern's shriek. It was sharper than the hunting cry of a golden hawk and more dangerous than the hiss of a king cobra, and it made everyone freeze in their tracks.

"Salem, do you really want to let your reception turn into a brawl?" I asked. My cousin shook his head and took a step away from Marus and Prentice. "Do you want that to be the memory your parents take with them when they leave tonight?" I was aware that my voice was less than warm, and

I didn't care. "Prentice, perhaps you should talk to Sive before you put her in the middle of a riot." Prentice's eyes widened, and he turned his head to locate his pair bond. Sive had pressed herself against the edge of the dais, trying to get out of the way of the crowd. "Marus. Urban. What happened?"

"Oliza, he . . ." Marus hesitated, as if realizing that his excuse was not enough to justify the fight. "I lost my temper."

"So I saw." I sighed. I doubted that Urban was entirely innocent. No doubt each of them had been trying to bait the other. Marus had just been unlucky enough to throw the first punch.

Marus stepped forward. "Oliza, you didn't hear—"

"Don't bother," Prentice said. "You're an avian and you hit a serpent. That's all anyone here cares to see."

"Prentice!" Sive exclaimed.

Prentice looked at his pair bond briefly, but his next words were for me. "Are you going to say otherwise?" he challenged. "Tell me it matters to you that the snake was making intentionally inflammatory remarks."

Urban protested. "I wasn't—"

"Or are you just going to say, 'That's their way,' and ignore it," Prentice continued, "the way you always ignore the culpability of serpents when their behavior becomes more than one of *us* can stand?"

"Thank you," Marus said respectfully to Prentice, "but you don't need to defend me. I could have walked away. I shouldn't have hit him." The words obviously pained him. I suspected that this, like the apology he had offered back on the avian hills, was a bow to my sensibilities and not an admission of his own beliefs.

"Urban hit back fast enough," Prentice muttered.

"Prentice, I think it's time we left," Sive suggested, taking his arm. "This is a private matter, and it seems to be under control."

As they left, I noticed that sometime during the argument the rest of the serpents had backed off as well.

Marus shrugged. "Even I know enough about serpiente culture to know that you don't hit one without expecting to be hit back."

"Either of you have anything else to say?" I asked.

They both shook their heads. "But I'm not going to volunteer to help any of your other suitors in the future," Urban said. "I don't know where I came up with that idea in the first place."

The night had been a fabulous disaster. Most serpiente would continue to celebrate for hours yet, but Urban spoke for all of us when he announced with obvious frustration, "It's been a long day. I'm going to bed."

He and Marus exchanged one last look, too tired to be quite hostile, before he turned back toward the nest.

"I'll see you in the morning, Oliza," Marus said hopefully.

I nodded, and he changed form and took wing back to his home in the northern hills.

I used the disruption both as an opportunity to pull Salem aside and summarize what Tavisan had told us and as an excuse to leave early without offending anyone. I had spent many nights curled in the arms of the dancers, enjoying their warmth and company, but that night quiet solitude was all I wanted.

CHAPTER 4

A t the last moment, I changed my direction so that instead of immediately going to the Rookery, I stepped
into the forest beyond the northern hills. I needed to calm
down before I would be able to sleep.

I was not surprised when Nicias landed by my side a moment later. He was my guard, and he would not leave me
alone, especially while there was any rumor of unrest among
the nearby wolves. He gave me distance as I picked my way
through the darkened woods, lost in thought, but he came to
me when I sighed.

"What happened?" he asked. "I saw your parents off and
then flew over the southern hills just in time to see you come
out here."

I briefly described the fight, trying to keep the bitterness
from my voice. After I was done, Nicias let a few moments
pass in awkward silence before asking softly, "Do you want to
talk, or should I give you space?"

Though I knew he could not go far enough for me to be
truly on my own, I appreciated the offer of privacy.

We had been friends for so long, I chose instead to tell him the fears that I rarely shared with anyone. "I love the serpiente, the dancers, the silken *melos* scarves and the Namir-da," I said. "I love the avians, their singers, the sky, the poetry and the philosophical debates in the northern side of the marketplace. I love both sides of Wyvern's Court . . . enough to admit that despite their sitting on opposite sides of a single valley, intended to be one society, they might as well sit on opposite sides of the world. They are two completely different civilizations, and neither wants to change to accommodate the other—and I don't feel I have the right to tell them to."

Nicias looked away, and I regretted how frustrated I had sounded. I tried not to burden others with these fears. I might have apologized, but before I could, he said, "You're right. But we've come so far by not killing each other. There *has* to be a way." Thoughtfully, he suggested, "Your parents went to the Mistari. Perhaps an outside perspective would help again?"

"Perhaps, but what if the tigers agree with all the others? The wolves don't understand why we bother to try; Kalisa and I had a long discussion about this when her pack was visiting the market a few months ago." Kalisa and I had always gotten along; I respected her. I hoped she was not as badly injured as the lions' message had indicated. "Kalisa said they respected our efforts but it isn't natural for two people who are so different to mesh. And the falcons?" Nicias winced.

"Think it can't be done," he said, as he had many times before. That was one of the very few things he had told me of his days on Ahnmik.

He would tell me the rest, if he ever thought I needed to know.

Nicias had seemed older since he had come home from the falcons' island four months before. When he had returned to Wyvern's Court, he'd had wounds that spoke of torture. Those injuries had since healed, but whatever he had learned had marked him permanently.

He had continued studying magic, but I had never met his teacher, and he seemed reluctant to speak of her. I had put enough together from his vague references to know that she worked with him from the city of Ahnmik, without needing to come physically to Wyvern's Court.

"What if I go to the Mistari, and they say the same thing?" I challenged. "It can't, or shouldn't, be done? People see the Mistari as almost infinitely wise. If I brought that message back with me, it would fracture the court further. I can't risk that kind of damage." But doing nothing meant risking the kind of damage that could have occurred that night. "Maybe I should just give it up," I said, joking. "Shock everyone and elope with a falcon."

There had never been anything between Nicias and me beyond friendship, and yet he tensed, moving away from me.

"Don't, Oliza," he said.

"Wyvern's Court isn't something I should joke about," I said, concurring. "I just get so frustrated."

"I know," he answered, "but it's not a safe joke to make, even in frustration. There are too many people who would take you seriously."

Too many people, in these woods? What had happened to the days when we could share our dreams and he didn't chastise me about the shadows overhearing us?

I frowned, hurt. I knew what would happen if I *did* take a falcon for my mate. Both serpiente and avians would probably rebel. I would have a civil war on my hands. Even if that wasn't the case, everyone knew that a falcon couldn't take a pair bond from another breed without the risk of having a child whose magic was too strong to control. Hai was a vivid example of that madness.

The impossibility was what made my friendship with Nicias safe. There had never been a chance for a relationship between us, so we could both tease and not worry about it going further.

I supposed he had stopped teasing after his trip to Ahnmik. I hadn't noticed until just then.

"It's late," Nicias said softly, "and it has been a long day. Maybe it would be best to face these questions in the morning."

I nodded. "You're right. It's too late tonight to make any decisions anyway, too late to do anything but turn over the same fears."

We said our farewells, and I changed shape and stretched my wyvern's wings, circling once over my home, as if to bid it good night. The dancers would keep the southern hills bathed in light and music until nearly dawn, but the rest of my world was quiet and peaceful.

Almost. Shifting shadows drew my attention to something out of place in the avians' northern hills, a figure lying on the ground, curled on its side on the cobblestone path between the houses. My pulse sped as I dove toward the unusual sight. It was common for people to sleep outside on the southern hills in good weather, but it was unheard of *there*, on the hard cobbles of the north.

I fell into human form near enough to make out dark

hair. Fair skin. Clothes that could pass for acceptable in either court. A *melos* tied around his waist, with a fringe of silver thread. A dancer.

Urban.

I tumbled to his side, skinning one knee when I saw the blood on him.

"*Urban!*" I shouted, but was afraid to touch him. He was curled in a protective ball, one arm over his head, his hair in his face so I couldn't see it. *Please don't let him be . . .* "Urban, *please . . .*"

Tentatively I touched his shoulder and turned him toward me, and though it made me cringe, the pained sound he let out was the sweetest thing I had ever heard. Thank the gods at least he was alive.

"Urban, it's me, Oliza. How badly are you hurt?" I was torn between wanting to stay with him and wanting to take to the skies to drag back a doctor *right then.*

A doctor, and guards. If someone had done this to him, it had happened just moments before. Whoever was responsible had to be nearby still. I couldn't leave Urban alone, unprotected.

"Oliz—" He hissed in pain and then slowly, agonizingly, tried to lift his head.

"Don't move yet," I told him. "I'll be right back."

I rose to my feet and shifted back into my wyvern form, propelling myself into the air, with one eye still on Urban. As I shot above the mist, I let out a shriek capable of shattering glass.

Within seconds, two of my avian guards took to the sky. Other avians rose from their beds and came to doorways. All the serpents who were celebrating in the southern hills, including Gretchen, looked up.

Half a minute had passed since I'd left Urban, but by the time I landed beside him again, I had six of my guards with me.

Nicias took charge. "Get to the Rookery and bring back a doctor *now;* I don't care who you have to wake up," he ordered two of the avians, who instantly returned to the sky. "The rest of you, spread out, try to find sign of who did this. Try not to panic people." Meanwhile, he knelt by Urban to assess the damage.

By this time, Gretchen had reached us, her face flushed from the run. "Oliza, what's—" She went pale when she saw Urban, but her first question was for me. "Oliza, are you all right?"

I nodded sharply, even though I understood why I had to be her priority. "I found him. I wasn't here when it happened."

"It's all right," Nicias was saying to Urban. "You're going to be all right." He lifted his gaze to me, and I could tell he was worried.

"Is there anything you can do?" I asked.

"I'll try."

He brushed the hair out of Urban's face, revealing bruises and a long cut down his cheek. One of Urban's eyes was swollen shut, but the other eventually focused on Nicias, and Urban cringed, perhaps anticipating the touch of what the serpiente considered falcons' black magic.

"It'll be all right," Nicias said again before he closed his eyes, drew a breath, and then went impossibly still.

By the time the doctor arrived a few minutes later, Urban's eyes had closed again, but he was breathing regularly. Nicias looked up, finally releasing the long breath he had held, and reported, "I can't do any more. I don't know how. I managed to stop the bleeding inside, but he has broken bones, things—" He pressed a hand to the ground as if to steady himself. "I'm not a trained healer."

The doctor, an avian named Rian, nodded. "I'll take care of him."

The next two hours were torture. I waited in the Rookery library, my head in my hands and my body shaking with adrenaline, while the doctor tended to Urban.

"Oliza?"

I looked up when I heard Gretchen. "Urban is awake. He wants to speak to you."

"How is he?"

"The doctor is . . . optimistic." The careful words made me pale, and she quickly clarified, "He'll live. But the doctor is avian. I do not think she understands that Urban is more concerned about the broken leg and the dislocated knee than he would have been about a potentially fatal injury."

"Gods," I whispered. Gretchen was not exaggerating. A dancer's craft was his life. Who had done this?

I stood to go, and Gretchen added hesitantly, "Urban also wants us to speak to the nest and bring a serpent here to stay with him."

I began to nod, surprised that Gretchen had even bothered to pass that request by me instead of simply fulfilling it, and then it hit me. When the dancers heard about the attack on Urban, they would be furious and assume that avians were to blame. We needed to find out who had done this before word got out, or the dancers might take matters into their own hands.

"I'll speak to Urban," I said, "and then we'll figure out the rest."

CHAPTER 5

"How is he?" I asked the doctor as she stopped me in the doorway of Urban's room.

"He'll make it," Rian said, "but not thanks to any craft of mine. Nicias minimizes his skill. Judging by the injuries I saw, if the falcon hadn't been on the scene, I'm not certain I would have been able to do anything. I know you'll need to talk to Urban, but make it quick. He needs rest now."

I didn't bother to try to explain that Urban would not be able to rest well until he was back in the nest and safe in the arms of his fellow dancers. That would be my problem. "Can he be moved?"

"If he must be, but he won't be able to walk. He'll need to stay off that leg for a week at least if he wants it to heal right."

She left the room, and I went to Urban's side. I had to bite my lip to keep from cursing when I saw him. I wanted to weep; I wanted to scream. *What kind of monsters could have done this?*

I forced myself to remain calm when I said, "I hate to have

to question you so soon, but I need to know what happened, before the rumors start."

"You mean," Urban said, "before the dancers learn that one of their people was jumped by a group of avians?"

I winced. "You're sure they were avian?"

"Yes."

"What happened?" I didn't want to know, but I needed to.

Urban shut his eyes and took a shaky half breath. "I'm not sure. A little while after you left, I walked over to the northern hills. Figured I should go by Marus's house to see if he was still awake, and apologize."

"Apologize?" I asked, impressed but surprised that he would have decided to do such a thing, especially since Marus had hit him first.

"I might have baited him—just a bit," Urban admitted.

"So you walked to the northern hills."

"There isn't much more to tell," he said. "I thought I remembered where Marus's house was, and I was on my way there. It was dark. I felt a couple of people nearby—avians." He didn't need to clarify how he knew they were avians. Serpiente were cold-blooded; if he had felt their body heat, they couldn't have been serpiente. "Someone hit me with something. . . . I don't know. I don't remember much more. I remember someone saying . . ."

"Go on."

"Just, 'Stay away from her,' " he mumbled. "I'm sorry."

"You're sorry?" I whispered. "Urban, this is my fault if—"

"It's not your fault. It's their fault." He coughed before muttering, "And they call us violent."

"Do you remember anything else about the people who attacked you?"

He shook his head and then cringed as if the movement

hurt. "I don't remember. There were two. Maybe three, but I think two."

"Marus?" I asked hesitantly. An even worse possibility . . . "Prentice?" Both had been directly involved in the violence earlier.

He started to smirk. "I'd love to say yes, but I don't know."

"I need to talk to my parents."

Had anyone sent for them? It had been only a few hours since they had left, but it would be difficult for even an avian to locate them until the sun was up.

Had any night ever been longer than this one?

"If the doctor says it's all right, I'd like to go back to the nest . . . but I'm going to need help."

I hesitated a little too long and saw his eyes widen.

"Oliza—"

"Will you wait until I talk to my parents?"

"Oliza, I've done nothing wrong."

"Of course you haven't—"

"If the nest learns that you refused to let one of their dancers go home—if you *lie* to them . . ."

I pressed a hand to my forehead. "You've done nothing wrong, and I have no intention of holding you against your will or lying to anyone. I am *asking* you to please wait until I have spoken to my parents and the Wyverns, so that I will have something to tell people."

"That wasn't meant to sound like a threat," Urban assured me. "I'm on your side. I'd like to wring the necks of the mangy fowl who hit me, but I can't stand the idea of letting them create a rift in the nest. Salem Cobriana was the first member of the royal house to join us in twenty generations.

Don't betray that—not to protect a bunch of birds too cowardly to even show their faces."

He was right. As much as I would have liked to keep this quiet until I had more answers, serpiente did not tolerate deception from their royal house. Too many people had seen me shout for help. Too many people would notice that Urban was missing, and would start asking about him, if they hadn't already.

"I won't." I stood up, touching his cheek gently on one of the few unbruised spots. "I'll be back as soon as I can, and I'll help you to the nest. In the meantime . . ." The promise that there would be guards on the door would be of little comfort. They weren't his nestmates, the people a serpent went to when hurt or scared.

"Hurry back."

"Gretchen, I want to see all the guards who examined the scene earlier," I told the python after I left Urban's room. "We need to get Urban back to the nest as soon as possible, and I want to know *something* before we do. I need to talk to Salem right away," I added. I would need him to help keep the dancers calm in the next few hours. "And then I'm going to need to speak to Marus and Prentice." That was going to be unpleasant. "And please get someone with wings who can find my parents." *Now*, I wanted to add, or better yet, *Yesterday*.

As Gretchen jumped to respond to my commands, I walked with rapid strides to one of the empty classrooms. I needed to get myself under control, needed . . .

I screamed, muffling the sound with a cushion so that my

guards wouldn't come running once again. There was no way to beat down this horror, this fury—this *terror*.

My fault, my fault. I wasn't the one who had hit Urban, but I was the one who had insisted he come to Festival. I was the one who had laughed and assured him he would be fine. I screamed again. I felt blind, and helpless.

"Don't do it."

The voice from the doorway made me jump. Hai. I turned toward her with a glare hot enough to melt steel. She looked back at me with an absolute lack of concern.

"Don't do what?" I asked when she did not speak again.

"I don't know. What are you about to do?"

I struggled to compose myself. "Hai, can you act sane for just a moment—please? I don't have it in me right now to play riddles."

"How nice for you."

"Hai—"

She made an abrupt motion, cutting me off. "A *sakkri* isn't neat like a letter. I was never trained; I can't control it. At least I remember mine. Most without training cannot."

"*Sakkri?*" I knew of them from my studies in the dancer's nest. The various forms of *sakkri* performed by serpiente were the remnants of ritual dances that had once been used to conjure powerful magic long ago. Some *sakkri* had called the rain; some had been used to create illusions; some had been prayers for divine assistance and some had summoned spirits of the past and future. There were dozens of varieties, some of which I had performed and many that I would not even begin to study for years yet.

Unlike the serpiente, the falcons had never lost their magic. My cousin, despite her cobra features, claimed to wield a falcon's ancient power. "Magic. Vision. *Sakkri'a'she.*"

She tried to explain. "You are about to do something that changes everything."

The *sakkri'a'she* was one of the more intricate *sakkri*, which I vaguely knew but had never performed. If one believed the stories, this particular form had been used to ask the future for guidance.

"How can you be warning me not to do what I'm about to do when I don't even *know* what I'm about to do?" I snapped.

"Your not knowing what the weather will be tomorrow does not change it."

"Presumably my knowing what I'm about to do would affect *that*."

Why was I arguing about this? I didn't believe in prophecy, and even if I had, I wasn't certain I would have trusted a prophecy told to me by my crazy cousin.

"Of course. This is why I came to speak to you." She waved a hand dismissively. "The mind barely comprehends its own yesterday, but *sakkri* force on it other times, other places, other people, visions it tries to shake away because to hold them all would only court madness. A single soul is not meant to know every *is* and *was* and *may be* and *could have been*. What I see is never as clear as *why* and *when* and *where* and *how*. Just pieces of a memory that aren't meant to be mine. All I know is that within the next few minutes, what you do—what you *did*, or will do, in the future I saw . . ." She closed her eyes and let out a heavy sigh. "I do not know."

Regardless of whether I believed her, I thought I understood the warning: consider carefully before acting. I needed to calm down so that I could think rationally.

"Thank you for trying," I said. "I will be careful."

She shook her head. "I hope so."

I closed my eyes and drew in a deep breath, meditating the way dancers did before a performance. Those mental exercises included envisioning the steps the body would soon take; now I forced myself to think of a plan for Wyvern's Court.

Urban was right that we could not put the dancers off for long, but it would be equally dangerous to speak to them without some kind of reassurance. *Damn* Kalisa for calling my parents away. How would I deal on my own with the only suspects we had so far?

Speaking to Marus would be hard enough. After all, he was a longtime friend. Worse, though, would be confronting Prentice. I doubted he would react well to the accusation. Avians considered themselves above the vulgar passions that led to violence; they would not want to believe that an alistair to the royal house could be responsible for such a vicious attack. If Prentice *wasn't* found guilty but word got to the serpiente that he had been questioned, they might jump to the conclusion that he had been protected because of his position.

There was no good way for this to end.

"Vemka!" I snarled a curse I had learned in the nest. *Calm down, Oliza. Calm down, and think of a plan.*

I opened my eyes. Hai was still there, watching me with an utterly inscrutable expression.

"Hai, thank you for your concern, but would you please leave and let me think?"

"If I thought you were capable of such, I would," she said, "but I live in this place, too, and I would rather it still be here tomorrow."

I needed something to calm my rioting, exhausting

thoughts. Prompted by Hai's warning, I chose the *sakkri'a'she*. *You're thinking too much about what you are doing*, my teachers always told me. *You aren't comfortable with it yet.* Right then, I needed something that would take all my concentration, something that would force my fears from my mind long enough for me to relax and step back.

I took another deep breath, calling to mind what the music would sound like, hearing the rhythm in my head before I began to focus all my attention on the subtle, tricky ripples of the dance. I was vaguely aware of Hai nearby; she sighed, and I remembered that she had once been a dancer herself. She took a step toward me.

If I had Hai's power, could I use this dance as my ancestors had, to beg the spirits of the future for guidance?

I felt at peace, as if all the world was held at bay for a moment.

But then it was as if I had been struck by lightning, and I found myself with my palms pressed against the ground, tears in my eyes, my whole body shaking, unsure of exactly where or when or who I was.

Hai recoiled from me. "Whatever you have just done, I'll thank you not to do it again," she choked out before stumbling from the room.

Whatever I had done . . . Thoughts lingered in my mind like a dream. I needed to—

This is madness–

I woke in the Rookery courtyard, to the sound of Nicias calling my name. An instant later he was beside me, whispering something in the old language that had to be a prayer.

"Where am I?"

"Are you hurt?"

"I—no. How long have I been—"

"*Oliza!*"

"I—what?" Gretchen was with us now, and Nicias sounded slightly frantic. He had put a hand on my shoulder, and I pushed it away. "I'm fine," I said. "I think."

My head was spinning. How had I gotten there? I remembered talking to Hai, and then . . . a vague sense of knowing I had to do something, go somewhere . . .

"You're pale," Nicias said. "Does anything hurt?"

I shook my head and pushed myself up—

I was standing; we were at the stairs to the Rookery. I was holding Nicias's arm for support.

"Oliza?" Gretchen asked when we paused abruptly.

I felt as if I had been dreaming and was waking up in stages. At least I remembered now when it had begun. "Remind me never to let Hai 'help' me again."

"What about Hai?" Nicias asked.

What about Hai? She had come to the library. "*Sakkri'a'she,*" I said. "She was talking about something I was going to do. She wasn't making any sense."

"*Sakkri'a'she* are rarely worked even on Ahnmik," Nicias explained. "Of all the versions of *sakkri,* the *a'she* is among the most difficult. It allows the user to see possible futures, ranging from those that are likely to occur, to those that could occur only if a very unlikely series of events took place. Falcons have been known to go mad struggling to fight Fate to bring about events that they would never have known could occur if they hadn't seen them. And Hai . . ." He sighed. "She has no way to control it. She has told me that she gets lost in time constantly. The past and the present and the future overlap in her mind, so sometimes she sees the consequences of her actions before she has even decided what to do, and sometimes she sees her own 'free will' as nothing more than a result of the choices of those who came before. You didn't try to perform one in her presence, did you?"

The concept made me shudder. I recalled thinking how valuable it would be to know what the future held, but I would never want to pay that price.

The deeper explanation of Hai's madness, though chilling, did not explain the loss of time I had experienced, and my lingering disorientation. As I recalled the strange, painful incident, Nicias went a shade paler.

"The magic that still lingers in the Cobriana line disturbs falcon magic; it acts like a spark," Nicias said, sounding shaken. "If Hai were already half-caught in a *sakkri'a'she* when you began to dance one, your being there might have triggered something. Or her being there might . . ." He trailed off. "I have to tell you something I've put off. It can wait until after we deal with Urban, but tomorrow, I need some time."

"Yes, of course."

He shook his head as if to clear it. "Salem, Sive, Prentice and Marus are all here, waiting for us—for you. Do you need to rest, or are you ready to speak to them?"

"I'm as ready as I'll ever be."

I wasn't losing time anymore, but the night continued to progress in a kind of haze. I felt as if there was something I was missing. My sense of frustrated ignorance was not helped by the meetings that followed.

None of the guards had seen anything. Marus and Prentice, both of whom had been pulled from their beds, seemed legitimately horrified as they swore their innocence. Salem first reacted as I feared all the dancers would—with pure fury, which he immediately directed toward Prentice—but he responded to my appeals that, in this, he needed to be a cobra first and a dancer second. We needed him on our side.

We had no proof of guilt, very few suspects and even fewer leads. The only concrete decision that we were able to make involved Urban and the nest.

"Salem and I will help Urban back to the nest and explain that we're doing all we can. We need to make sure that the dancers know we're on their side so no one will think about taking justice into their own hands. We can't afford vigilante retaliation. My parents should be here soon. They . . ." What could they possibly do to make things right?

Nothing can make this right.

CHAPTER 6

Urban, Salem and I were welcomed into Wyvern's Nest with anxious eyes and horrified questions. Rumors about what had happened had already reached the southern hills, and the only way we could calm people at all was to beg them to be quiet for Urban's sake, so that he could rest.

Salem helped Urban to a comfortable spot near the central fire as I faced the questions I had anticipated. *Who did it? Were they avians? Was it Prentice? Of course it was Prentice; everyone knows he hates dancers. Was it Marus? Everyone saw him hit Urban earlier. Will the attacker be turned over to the serpiente for nest justice?* Everyone had a theory and a proposed solution. Urban freed me from the interrogation; Salem took over for me, as if he had not nearly come to blows with Prentice in the Rookery just minutes before.

I joined Urban on the pallet of blankets and cushions that the other dancers had put together in front of the fire. Mindful of his injuries, I nevertheless lay as close to him as I could without pressing against him, knowing that he would want that comfort even more after having been denied it among the avians.

Almost immediately, he shifted to close the distance, my warmth and companionship more important than bruises.

I only meant to lie down for a few minutes, but the night had been too long. I didn't even realize I had fallen asleep until a wolf's howl startled me awake.

Urban woke when I stirred, and he asked, "Something wrong?"

"No," I answered. "Just the wolves. Go back to sleep; you need the rest."

"I've been 'resting.' " He shifted and winced. "I don't think that doctor remembered that she was talking to a dancer when she told me to stay off my feet for a week. I feel like I'm going to crawl out of my skin if I don't move, and it's only been a few hours."

Carefully, I put an arm around him. Worse than the doctor's orders to stay off the injured leg, no doubt, was her warning that it might not heal right if he didn't.

He sighed and closed his eyes again to sleep. As I did the same, he ran an idle hand through my hair, tickling the feathers at the nape of my neck. It reminded me of when we had been children, curled together in the nest at the end of a day of mischief. He had always been fascinated by my feathers.

"Oliza?"

"Hmm?"

"I . . . never mind." He sighed.

I opened my eyes and saw in his gaze something unchildlike.

Abruptly the mood changed. Though I knew that Urban considered himself one of my foremost suitors, I had always seen him as a friend, nestmate, safe companion when the rest of the world was cruel. That safer world fractured into sharp, fragile pieces as he turned my head so that he could steal a very *adult* kiss.

I pulled away instinctively. "Stop."

I had no doubt that he would, no fear. He smiled sadly, knowing the answer before he asked, "Don't suppose you're just saying that because I'm injured and you're worried about hurting me?"

I shook my head.

"Can't blame me for asking." In the space left between us, the night air suddenly felt colder.

A few minutes crept by in near silence, broken only by the chattering of predawn birds, as we both pretended to return to sleep. I don't think it surprised him when I stood up, saying, "I'm going to see if my parents are back yet."

Not far away, Salem was watching us. Rousing Rosalind, who had been curled against his chest, he hurried to meet me before I reached the doorway.

"I need to see if there is any news," I said. "I shouldn't have stayed as long as I did."

Salem sighed. "Good luck. Urban's not just any dancer. He grew up in Wyvern's Nest; he's like everyone's little brother."

"Which means he's going to have a lot of big brothers looking for payback," I said. "I know."

"Oliza . . ."

"Yes?"

"He *is* a good man. Don't let a bunch of thugs scare you off."

If only it was that easy. "I have to go. Take care of him."

"We will."

As I paused at the doorway to glance back, Salem and

Rosalind repositioned themselves so that they bracketed Urban. He wouldn't be alone.

Once outside the nest, I walked silently toward town. My parents would have come to the nest if they were back, but I could still go to the Rookery to see if anyone had learned anything. Maybe there had been a witness. Maybe . . . maybe so many things that seemed unlikely.

I had just needed to get out of there.

I touched a hand to my lips.

My parents had married for politics and then fallen in love. If I had to do the same, would I be as lucky as they were? I wondered how many generations of ruler had made the same decision.

As if to match my bleak thoughts, the clouds opened up and the first spatter of rain landed just as I crossed the market center.

I walked quickly across the green marble plaza in which the symbol of *Ahnleh* was combined with an equally ancient avian sigil, the Seal of Alasdair, and paused before the white marble statue that stood at the center: a true wyvern, slightly taller than I was, its tail curled around the base, its wings spread proudly, and its head raised as it shouted to the sky. It had been built the year that I had been born, when the idea that avians and serpiente could live together was new and so many had been filled with hope.

I couldn't remember what it felt like to be that proud and sure. Maybe one could manage it only when caught in the coldness of stone. I stared at the wyvern, envying her, as I let my body shift into *my* half form.

The wings that tumbled down my back were the same color as the feathers at my nape, varying from gold to rusty red to nearly black; the snakeskin that covered my body from my ankles to my neck was black with a red sheen. My eyes shifted to a deep amber, the whites disappearing and the pupils becoming slit; my fangs were filled with a cobra's poison.

My full wyvern form was similar to the statue, but this was my half form, my monster, a form no one I knew could see without flinching.

I leaned against the cold marble wyvern, putting my arms around her lithe body.

In half form, my senses were almost as keen as those of a pure cobra and those of a hawk combined. That was why I heard the sound of bare feet slipping slightly across the rain-slicked marble plaza floor, and why I felt the body heat of several creatures suddenly surround me. I turned to flee or fight, but I had no chance to even recognize my attackers before their hands slammed me back into the statue. One of my wings smacked into the ridge of its back, and I gasped as I felt bones break, my vision wavering so that the figures around me were nothing but vague outlines in the rainy morning.

Before I could recover, one of my attackers grasped my wrists, and others extended my wings without care for the broken bones. The pain made my stomach roll and I choked back bile.

"I'm sorry," said a voice that seemed familiar as I felt a blade begin to cut my long flight feathers.

My gasps were halted as someone put a cloth over my mouth and nose, muffling me and cutting off my breathing until I spiraled into unconsciousness.

CHAPTER 7

Time passed in an odd, warped way, so that I could not tell how long I was in my strange, rocking prison, less than half-awake. Sometimes I would open my eyes and there would be light; sometimes it would be dark as pitch. Most of the time, my vision was too blurry to tell any more than that.

The first time I woke with any true awareness, I found myself lying on my stomach in human form, though I did not remember returning to it. I tried to shift, and the combination of pain and dizziness forced me to stop and cry out as I clutched at the wooden planks beneath me.

Sometime later I came to again. My world wasn't swaying as badly, but my head was pounding and my mouth felt cottony. People were talking nearby in loud voices, which seemed to warp and waver, swirling in the air. Someone asked, "Can't we let the princess out now?"

"This whole area is infested with wolves," someone else responded. The voice . . . I knew that voice. "No need to let them see her."

There was a pause; then someone else said, "She's moving around again."

"Bring her something to eat and drink." The speaker was Tavisan, the leader of the lion mercenaries. But why had they done this? Had the wolves hired them? Kalisa wouldn't have; who were her rivals? I did not know what might benefit them.

The wall of my tiny little room was peeled back, letting in a bit of light from their fire. The lion who blocked the doorway was broad shouldered, and his gaze never left me as he put a canteen of water and a plate of simple food in front of me.

"Wait!" I called after him as he started to move away. My voice cracked; my throat was so dry. He ignored me and carefully fastened the leather wall back into place. "Tavisan!"

I could barely speak above a whisper. I grabbed the canteen of water and chugged half of it before I even noticed the smell of roasted meat. Starving, I shoved food into my mouth. I needed strength to . . .

Needed to . . .

The thought drifted away. Woozy, I lay down again, and belatedly the word came to mind: *drugged.*

When I slept, my dreams were hazy visions not just of home but of whatever fate I was going toward. At one point, I woke, screaming, from a nightmare about butterflies.

"Milady, I cannot possibly—"

"Tavisan, please."

When I fell asleep again, the image changed to Urban,

bleeding—and then it was Marus instead. Sometimes others; sometimes all of Wyvern's Court. The dancer's nest was on fire. Sometimes there were falcons, and occasionally lions.

I knew I had to get away. To *run*. Far away, because someone had me, and they weren't afraid to use violence—I remembered my wing breaking—or to drug my food. The haziness left from the drugs made it impossible for me to concentrate for very long, and I struggled to keep from drowning in fear.

Finally I woke fully enough to realize that I was inside some kind of covered litter. The walls and the top were leather, and they were attached so firmly to the heavy wood floor that in my weakened state I could not pry them away. I still worked at it, trying to ignore the way my stomach rolled with every movement, and I nearly collapsed as the vertigo hit me.

The drugs were in the water, I decided. I had to stop drinking it, to clear my mind so that I could make a plan instead of continuing this useless scratching.

Eventually it occurred to me that mercenaries worked for payment. Surely Wyvern's Court could offer the lions more than their current employers—and if prizes would not work, a pride of lions was not stronger than the serpiente and avian armies.

"Tavisan!" I shouted again. "You know who I am. Talk to me. We can work something out." I waited but heard no response. "Tavisan, you were in Wyvern's Court the day before I was taken. When my people find that I am gone, they will quickly discover your role in my abduction. Is the payment you have been offered enough to risk the wrath of Wyvern's Court?"

I heard whispering among the lions carrying my litter then.

"Tavisan, she has a point. Wyvern's Court—"

"I know what I'm doing." The leader's voice was certain.

"But what if—"

"Do not question me," he snapped.

"Tavisan, you are destroying your own people," I argued. I had a vague memory of arguing with him before. How many times had I woken, in my drugged state, and perhaps said these exact words?

"Oliza, I apologize for your rough treatment. I wish it had not been necessary. Even so, you are wasting your breath."

I continued to call to him, alternating between threats and promises, sometimes trying to bargain with Tavisan and sometimes appealing to his people, but I received no more answers. Eventually my throat was again too raw to continue shouting, and I dared not drink to soothe it.

I avoided the drugs long enough to clear my mind, but after two days without water, the cramping in my body became so severe, I knew that dehydration might kill me. I curled up in a ball in the corner of the litter, trying to concentrate on something productive.

They had clipped my wings. They had clipped my wings and then fed me a poison to force me back into my human form. I knew the process because it was one of the most severe punishments meted out in avian society.

It permanently locked someone out of both her half- and full-avian forms. Locked me from my wings. My serpiente form would be unaffected, but my hawk was gone.

Grounded, forever. There was no cure; there never had been. That was why the avians used it as a final punishment, and only for the most extreme crimes.

Stop it, STOP IT! I tried to force the thoughts away.

Suddenly the ground was tilting, and I heard yelling, mostly in a language I did not know. Howls, shouts, sounds of fighting. My litter swayed again as whoever was holding it stumbled.

Instinctively, I threw myself to the side that was tilting. The impact of my body against the wood made me see stars, but I did it again, and again—

Until my litter tipped and hit the ground *hard,* one side splitting as the wood broke with a crack as loud as a thunderclap. I blacked out for a moment but was too frantic to do anything but drag myself up afterward. I crawled through the split, gasping at the cold outside. Instantly soaked, I forced myself to move. Water, on my hands; I licked it off gratefully.

I didn't know who was fighting, and I didn't waste time looking. With the drugs slowing me down, I rose to my feet, sprinted, stumbled, rolled as I fell and fought to my feet again. *Woods.*

The forest looked like a haven and I scrambled into it, cutting open my hands, knees and arms on brambles in my mad flight.

Later I collapsed, choking on my own heavy breathing; body cramping, demanding water, food and sleep. I could give it two of those. There was water everywhere; I scooped it up in my aching, frozen hands. Cold.

Sleep.

I hoped I wouldn't be found. I curled up to conserve as much heat as I could, but I wasn't even shivering anymore. That was good, I decided. Not so cold now.

Sleep.

It felt as if days had passed, but all I knew for sure was that the sun was out when I opened my eyes and sneezed on fur that was across my face. There was some animal next to me, giving me its warmth. I had enough clarity of mind now to realize that the creature—a wolf, I realized as I turned—was the only reason I *had* woken. I must have been on the verge of freezing to death when I had fallen asleep.

Snow. That was why there was water everywhere. I had seen snow once, when I had gone with the Vahamil pack far to the north, but that had been nothing like this. This was deep and thick and still falling from the gray sky above.

I looked at the wolf, not for an instant believing that it was a wild beast, though unable to tell if it was from the pack with which I was familiar.

"Thank you," I said, shivering.

The wolf tilted its head, questioning.

I could feel the human in it—in *her*—and I knew that my savior was a shapeshifter. But she was looking at me without any human comprehension. "My name is Oliza. You saved my life, I think."

The wolf stood up and started plodding away from me. I stayed where I was, and she paused, looking back. She didn't need to speak; her warm brown eyes seemed to laugh at me, saying, *Follow.*

Where was I? I could remember only the last couple of days with the lions, after I had stopped taking the drugs, but the change in weather was drastic enough to make me think that we had traveled weeks away to the north. Weeks that I had been away from home, weeks during which my people should have come after me and found me.

I was too lost, and too weak, to travel on my own. So I followed my silent guide, though my steps dragged and my stomach rumbled. The drugs still felt thick in my system; I was perspiring even as I shivered, the winter air slicing through my clothes and freezing my sweat. The world kept turning to fog around me, but whenever I drifted, the wolf was there, bumping into my legs and guiding me in the right direction.

When I stopped, unable to move any farther, the wolf nudged me into a hollow where the snow was not so thick and the wind could not reach. She brought down a rabbit and we shared it, the raw meat disgusting to the "civilized" part of my mind but a welcome meal to the sensible, *starving* one.

My guide did not let me sleep. I suspected that she was worried I would not wake. After our meal I dragged myself back to my feet and we kept walking.

I spoke to the wolf as I walked. My stories were disjointed and often trailed off as I forgot what I had been saying, but my mute guide didn't complain. She made no indication that she understood, but the words helped keep me focused.

"I walked away, that was the last thing I did," I said, thinking of Urban. "He was hurt because of me but . . . I couldn't stay . . ."

Why had no one come for me? They had to know that the lions had taken me.

"My Wyverns. Gretchen, and Nicias—did I tell you about Nicias?" I thought I had. I had talked about magic . . . or something, earlier . . . "My best friend," I whispered. "The only man in Wyvern's Court not related to me who I can be alone with without causing a scandal. Shouldn't be a scandal." I had never been tempted to do anything scandal worthy. Oliza Shardae Cobriana, her mind always on her throne. It might have been nice to be a carefree child for a while, chasing butterflies in the summertime.

I envied Salem and Rosalind. What I wouldn't have given to look at someone with—"they love each other so much." Had I said the beginning of that thought aloud?

I was getting confused. I was repeating myself at times, but other times, I knew I was saying only fragments of sentences.

"I need sleep," I said. "I'm so tired."

I stumbled, going to my knees in the snow. My legs were numb. At least they didn't hurt.

The wolf nuzzled my shoulder with a whine. I put a hand on her shoulder and pushed myself back to my feet.

"It would be nice to be in the nest now," I mused. "A fire to keep warm. People around. Sometimes it drives me crazy. Serpiente don't believe in privacy, and it gets so that even your thoughts don't feel like your own, but it would be nice to be warm. Nice if Marus and Prentice didn't look horrified when . . ."

I realized I had stopped walking again only when the wolf bumped against the backs of my knees. She whined, trotted ahead a few paces and tossed her head in a way that made me look at the horizon.

The fires burning in the distance were the sweetest signs I had ever seen. Desperation gave way to hope, and I started moving faster, stumbling forward because I couldn't run with legs that had gone numb hours before.

Someone saw me and called out, and in that moment, my energy fled me. I had held on to it only because the wolf had demanded I keep walking. Poison, malnutrition, dehydration, exhaustion, cold and injuries caught up to me just in time for me to collapse into the arms of a young man I had never seen before.

CHAPTER 8

I woke warm and dry, if still a little woolly-headed. A fire was crackling, and as I opened my eyes, I found myself inside a small cedar hut decorated with furs, leathers and odd silver and bead ornaments. I sat up slowly, glad that the world did not spin too much, and looked around for the owner.

He sat in the corner, wrestling with some bit of leather that refused to do what he wanted. Intent on that project, he had not yet noticed that I was awake.

What if I wasn't safe? For all I knew, this was the mercenaries' destination. If Kalisa's rivals were responsible for my abduction, it would have made sense for them to place me in the power of their own allies—who were probably wolves.

I didn't know what I would do if these people were unfriendly. I thought about the weather outside.

And the wolf who had saved my life.

"Hello?" I said tentatively.

The man in the corner looked up and smiled. His striking amber eyes—which I had only ever seen on wolves—gave away his breed. Remembering how the wolf outside had not talked to me during our journey, I wondered if these people spoke a language I knew.

He paused a moment before answering. "Hello. Are you feeling better?" He had a heavy accent, but I could understand him easily enough.

I tottered to my feet a little unsteadily, but once I was up, the ground stayed solid. "Much better. Do I have you to thank?"

He gave a little shrug. "You have Fate to thank, for taking you to the edge of our camp. You were half-frozen, and poisoned. It is not all gone. Our doctor is not sure what it was. Eat well, stay warm, rest for a few days." He shrugged again. "You will be better."

"What about the wolf?" I asked. He looked amused, so I clarified. "Another wolf. I was farther away. One of your people saved my life; she brought me here."

"Ah," he answered. There was a long pause, and I did not think he would say more, but then he sighed. "That was Betia, perhaps. She is . . . feral?" he said hesitantly, as if unsure that he had translated right.

I nodded, unnerved. When a shapeshifter went feral, it meant that she had spent too much time in animal form. Eventually the human characteristics eroded, along with the memory of her original form. Usually a feral shapeshifter was volatile, without an animal's sense of balance or a human's sense of morals, prone to attack those who had been closest to her.

"Has no one tried to bring her back?" I asked. "She did not seem too far gone to me."

He shook his head. "Betia was my sister. I have tried all I could think of, but she lets no wolf speak to her, or touch her. She had a falling out with the alpha's son, Velyo," he confided, "and she ran away. I do not know what the fight was about, only that her animal mind associates our kind with

59

pain now. So she will not let us near." Again he shook his head, admitting, "It should be my job to hunt her down like an animal for the safety of the pack. But I can't, and so far our alpha has not forced me to."

The door opened, letting in a gust of cold air and an older woman who was speaking swiftly in a language I did not recognize.

The woman was plump in a comfortable sort of way and carried a bundle that smelled wonderfully like food. The man I had been talking to winced and nodded as she seemed to berate him.

Finally he turned to me. "My mother says that she is glad to see you awake, that I should not have let you get up, that she has brought breakfast, that I should have offered you something to eat and that she is sure my manners are terrible and I have not introduced myself or told you where you are." He smiled and then continued obediently. "I am Pratl; I am head huntsman. This is my mother, Ginna; she is doctor, advisor and anything else she believes is her role. Right now, you are in the huntsman's hut of the Frektane tribe. I believe it means *blue eyes* in your language."

I knew the name. Wyvern's Court had never traded directly with the Frektane, but the Vahamil occasionally brought their wares to our market. I wondered where the pack's name came from; I had never seen a wolf with blue eyes.

Another round of commentary from Ginna, and Pratl sighed. "Now I am talking too much. May I ask your name?"

I had to conclude that these people were friendly; they had given me help, and I had certainly needed it. So I answered honestly. "Oliza Shardae Cobriana. Arami, and heir to the Tuuli Thea."

Apparently Pratl's mother had understood at least some

of that, because her eyes widened and she stared at me. Then she shrugged—and continued talking.

Pratl laughed. "My mother says we are flattered to have you in our camp, even if you did . . ." He paused, working on the wording. "Did get dragged in from the blizzard looking like a winter rat. What brings you to our camp in such a condition?"

"Honestly, I am very lost," I answered.

Pratl frowned. "You weren't with that group of lions we intercepted?"

"Were you the ones who attacked them?"

He bristled. "Of course. They did not ask permission to hunt on our land, they were loud enough to scare away all the game for miles and their reputation is as foul as their mange-spotted coats. If you are with them—"

I held up a hand, shaking my head. "No, not like that. I was brought here by them. Against my will. I escaped when something attacked them—your pack, I assume." His vehement response comforted me. If this pack had been involved in hiring the mercenaries, Pratl at least had not known the plan.

He nodded, content now. "I believe that. I did not know who you were when we first found you, but I did not think any bird would be with them," he said, gesturing toward the feathers on the nape of my neck that must have made him assume I was avian even before I woke.

"How far am I from Wyvern's Court?" I asked, dreading the answer. How many days had I been traveling, semiconscious, while people from home had been searching for me?

Pratl conferred briefly with his mother before turning back to me and shaking his head. "The Frektane visit Wyvern's Court rarely, though some of our people winter with the Vahamil. It is probably not a long flight." He considered. "Maybe three weeks, traveling by land."

"*Three weeks?*" I gasped. I had feared that I had been drugged for that long, but I had hoped otherwise.

The lions had asked to trade in our market after they had delivered Kalisa's message. Had they been hired by someone while they had been in Wyvern's Court? I still did not know who had attacked Urban. What if the same culprit was responsible? And how could I take three weeks to get home?

"Lions travel quickly—faster than you would if you walked. But by air the time will be much less." He was right. I could probably travel that distance in a day, two at most . . . if I had my wings. I didn't have my wings.

Ginna interrupted with some sharp words to her son and started opening the bag she had brought.

"Breakfast," Pratl said simply. "She is concerned that if you get weak, the poison will make you sick again."

"Tell her thank you, please."

Pratl conveyed this, and then Ginna left us as Pratl and I sat down to eat.

"And thank you, for acting as translator," I added. "How is it that you know our language so well?"

As I ate with an appetite I had not expected, Pratl explained, "Among my pack, there is someone who studies each culture we might deal with, so that we can speak with them. Mostly we deal with Wyvern's Court through the Vahamil, but it is best to be able to speak for ourselves if we need to. My sister had that post, until recently. She taught me most of what I know. Our alpha's son saw your feathers, so he had you put here. He and his father are the only others in this area who speak your language besides me. Frektane will expect me to be able to tell him who you are, why you are here and how long you wish to remain with us."

From dealing with the wolf tribe near Wyvern's Court, I

knew that the leader of a pack was formally addressed by the pack name. The formality was often dropped among Kalisa's people, but apparently Frektane's alpha did not allow such familiarity.

"Frektane does not like strangers, but his son argued that it would be unwise to leave an unknown guest out in the snow. Now that we know who you are, I think Frektane will listen to his son."

Pratl's mother returned then with a bundle of clothing and a pair of fur-lined boots. She said something brief to him, and he nodded.

"Your clothes are not designed for this area, or for travel," Pratl told me. "These were Betia's. They should fit you, and you may keep them when you leave."

"How long has she been lost?" I asked.

Pratl winced. "Four months."

"So there's still hope for her."

"No," he sighed, and stood without elaborating. "Frektane is expecting you. Dress, and I will be back to take you to him."

I was happy to have the warm, dry clothing. The base of the outfit was a pair of wool pants and a loose, comfortable shirt of the same material. A heavy jacket, lined with some kind of fur, laced over the blouse. I pulled the boots up over the pants to just beneath my knees; they too were fur lined, amazingly warm and comfortable. Once I was ready, Pratl escorted me to the largest hut at the center of the camp, to meet with the leader of the Frektane. I could only hope that Pratl was right and I would be allowed to stay; I did not know what I would do otherwise.

CHAPTER 9

Frektane was still physically young, his body lean, but his face was marked by a series of scars across his left cheek and brow. I had never seen a wolf with such striking blue eyes; they had to be the reason for the tribe's name. If I had not been raised among serpents and falcons, whose eyes were often jeweled tones seen nowhere else in nature, I would have called such eyes impossible.

"Oliza Shardae Cobriana," Frektane greeted me stiffly.

"Forgive my father for not standing," another man said, making me jump as I noticed him for the first time. Also whipcord lean and obviously strong, and with the same vivid blue eyes as Frektane, this had to be his son, Velyo. "He injured his leg earlier this winter, and it still pains him."

The words were polite, but something about his tone made me feel as if an insult had been spoken.

Frektane responded by instantly rising to his feet. "My son makes much of a minor ailment," he responded, glaring at the younger wolf before he turned to me.

Sensing an argument I did not know the heart of, I did

my best not to get into the middle of it. "If I have come at an awkward moment, I apologize."

"My father and I were simply discussing . . . matters of little importance," Velyo answered. His father said something to him in their native tongue, and he smiled. "Kind, Father, of you to offer. But since I was the one who insisted we let Oliza stay, I will assume full responsibility for her."

"How long *are* you here?" Frektane asked me, ignoring Velyo.

"I was brought into this area against my will," I explained. "I fear traveling too soon may make me sick again. If it is not a hardship, I ask your permission to remain for a few days, until I am stronger."

Frektane made a disgusted sound, but before he could speak, Velyo assured me, "A few days will prove no hardship for us."

Again Frektane grumbled to his son in their language. This time, Velyo replied, "You are alpha, leader of this land and its people. Say the word, and I will see to it that *everyone* too weak to provide for the pack is removed."

He had hit a nerve, for suddenly Frektane crossed the room, favoring his right leg just slightly. "Watch yourself, Velyo."

"You're weak, Father," Velyo snarled. "This winter has been good to the pack, because *I* have led the hunts down the river. Hunts your injury kept you from. Before you talk of denying Oliza a few days to rest, consider how many of our resources you devour. You've been slower every run this season. The cold is in your bones. You're *old*, wolf."

I jumped back as Frektane threw Velyo into the wall. "Not old enough that a pup like you can challenge me."

Velyo snarled at his father as he pushed himself back to

his feet; then he glanced at me. "I'll escort Oliza while she is here."

"See that you do."

"I apologize for that little scene," he said, as if I had witnessed some minor spat, instead of part of an ongoing power struggle between father and son. "You may think our ways harsh, but in this kind of world, it is necessary to rule firmly. Laxity is what causes a pack to starve in the winter. My father's strength has been failing since he was injured last fall. I won't let him bring our entire pack down by refusing to admit it."

"I suppose I'm lucky to live in a more moderate climate," I answered, trying to remain polite despite my desire to argue. The wolves had different values than I did. As Velyo had said, this pack lived in a difficult land, where strength was necessary for survival. "Wyvern's Court has never had problems with starvation, for which I am grateful."

Velyo nodded. I couldn't tell if it was in agreement or approval or neither.

I wondered how Kalisa was doing. If she had needed my parents' support, what had happened when they had suddenly been pulled back to Wyvern's Court to deal with events there after I had disappeared?

Velyo seemed to be waiting for me to speak again, so I searched for a safe, neutral question. "How many people are in Frektane? It seems so quiet."

"Few more than a dozen winter here," he answered. "The weaker ones separate and travel south, nearer to your court. They trade among the human cities or stay with other, more southern packs. You have probably seen them with the

Vahamil, though I imagine your position leaves you little time to idle with common wolves. In spring or summer they will return here to the main encampment."

"What about the children?"

"They travel if they are old enough," he answered. "Otherwise, they stay here and people such as Ginna take care of them. Mostly they stay out of the way. Father does not like for them to get underfoot." Wyvern's Court had such a different opinion about children that I could not immediately think of an appropriate answer. Luckily Velyo chose that moment to offer, "If you would like to get word to your people, our relations with the Vahamil are good enough that they would not object to our sending a messenger through their lands to Wyvern's Court. You can wait here until your guards arrive to see you safely home."

"I would appreciate that," I said, and felt some of the tension in my neck begin to dissolve. A messenger from the Frektane could travel more quickly than I would be able to even in perfect health, which meant that my people would hear from me sooner. It had already been too long. "Do you know anything about Kalisa's condition? She was injured shortly before I was taken from Wyvern's Court."

"Injured?" Velyo asked. "I hadn't heard. Do you know how serious it is?"

I shook my head. "Serious enough that she wanted to meet with my parents, but I don't know more than that."

"Perhaps I will accompany you when you travel south, to check in on Vahamil." His thoughtful tone gave me a chill before his expression cleared. "In the meantime, join me for some dinner. You look half-starved."

The main encampment of the Frektane tribe was a very somber place, especially compared to the Vahamil's near my home. In addition to despising little children running about, making noise and getting underfoot, the alpha also disapproved of "frivolous" activities such as dancing and singing, which had always kept Kalisa's tribe active and alight with laughter.

"Someone will bring my father his supper. He prefers to eat in solitude," Velyo explained to me as we entered a central hut where the air was filled with the scents of roasting meats.

A young woman tended the hearth, but she stood the instant she saw Velyo, brushing ash from her hands. Two others sat at a long table in the back of the room, and they also stood hastily.

"This is Lameta's first winter in Frektane," Velyo told me, nodding to the hearth mistress. He greeted her in their native language, and she gave a half curtsy, never looking away from him. There was respect in her eyes, but I could tell she was also wary. I tried to keep an open mind, though from what I had seen and heard so far, I would not have wanted to be one of Frektane's and Velyo's subjects. They ruled with a fist that was a little too iron for my comfort.

We were served roast venison, with a warm, sweet sauce, and hot spiced wine.

"I'll warn you, meals in the winter can be somewhat repetitive," Velyo said apologetically. "I suspect Lameta dipped into the fruit stores tonight after she heard we had company."

As we turned to sit at the table, the two who had been sitting there went to serve themselves. Others came in from outside, as if they had been waiting for a dinner bell, and finally Lameta herself took a plate.

They had been waiting for Velyo, I realized. The pack didn't eat until its alpha had taken his share. I knew that law from my studies, though it was one of many that Kalisa enforced only in formal situations. Usually she preferred to give the first share to whichever hunter or tradesman had contributed the most to the meal.

"I have never been to your Wyvern's Court," Velyo said. "Tell me of it?"

I did my best to describe my homeland, from dancers to singers, merchants to scholars. Velyo listened quietly, nodding occasionally or quirking a brow when I said something he found curious.

"Do you have a mate waiting for you at home?" he asked finally.

His tone was innocent enough, but there was something about the way he looked at me that made my skin crawl, as if a hundred spiders had suddenly scampered across it.

"I have not yet chosen my king," I answered.

"I had forgotten that your people are born to royalty, or marry into it. It is a precious luxury."

"I assume that the alpha position in the Frektane must be hereditary, since the pack's name obviously refers to your line."

He sounded as if he was reciting as he explained, "It is not a matter of birthright, but breeding and education. If one of my wolves proves himself better qualified to lead the Frektane after my father no longer can, I will have to step down, but like my father, and his before him, throughout my childhood I was given the lessons I would need to take over as alpha once it is time. For nine generations we have led this pack, each Frektane alpha choosing a strong mate who will add worthy qualities to the bloodline. My mother could bring down a wild boar in her human form while armed with no more than a dagger. She could track antelope through pouring rain, and shoot an owl from the sky in the dead of a moonless night. My father has done a great many unwise things in his life, but choosing his mate was not one of them. I only hope I can choose a mate who will prove as fine a queen as my mother was.

"She truly earned the right to run by my father's side. It is good that she did not live to see him in his current state." He hesitated, then added, "Though at least she would have had the courage to put him down."

I had no desire to address the possible euthanasia of a man who by my standards was perfectly healthy. No wonder Kalisa had called her allies to her side when she had been injured, if this was how neighboring packs—not to mention her own—would view her weakness.

I steered the conversation back to a topic I understood all too well; I was the heir of not just one but two monarchies, and I understood the care that had to be taken in choosing a mate. "Have you made your decision?" I asked

"No." He stood up abruptly, without bothering with the dishes. Someone would clean up after him, I was sure. "There are women in the Frektane who are good hunters, women who are good leaders, women who are intelligent and women who are brave. It is rare that one finds all those traits in a single place. I thought I had once, but . . . I was incorrect."

Betia? I wondered. Pratl had said that she had had a falling out with Velyo. But the look in Velyo's eyes warned me not to inquire further.

CHAPTER 10

I was exhausted from my travels, even more tired by how carefully I had tried to watch my words with Velyo, and worried I had accentuated Kalisa's troubles by revealing her possible vulnerability. I was relieved when Velyo offered to escort me back to my room, because I would be able to rest.

The doorway was covered by heavy furs, and Velyo brushed them aside, allowing me to slip through the narrow opening. Someone had built the fire up before we arrived, so the room was warm despite the winter chill outside.

Velyo followed me inside and then, as if just deciding, said, "I think I'll join you."

"Excuse me?"

Had he been serpiente, accustomed to sleeping innocently among friends, I might have assumed that his offer was platonic, but as far as I was aware, the wolves did not share that particular custom.

He walked toward me, his stride graceful and soundless. "I said, I think I'll join you. It's a cold night."

I took a step back, but the room was small, and I only succeeded in hitting the backs of my knees on a trunk that sat at the foot of the bed. "I'm sorry if I somehow gave the wrong impression, but—"

He caught my hand and kissed the back of it. "You are half serpiente, are you not?"

Insulted, I fought the urge to deliver an equally offensive and thus hardly politic reply. Instead I used his own logic against him. "I am also half avian."

He shrugged. "You are also a guest in my camp. I thought you would be grateful."

"I am grateful," I answered, trying unsuccessfully to take my hand back. "However, I also—"

He stepped forward despite my protests, trapping me against the trunk. "You also?"

"Let go of me."

"Relax," he whispered.

"I am not interested," I said bluntly, feeling my heart trapped in my throat. "Now kindly release me."

I caught his wrist when he reached for me with his other hand, which made him chuckle a little. "Princess—" He yanked his hand back as he tugged on my wrist, so I ended up stumbling and falling against his chest. "I'm not sure you appreciate your position. There are many women who would be jealous of—"

"I'm not one of them," I growled. The last of my respect for him had disappeared, and with it my trust that he wouldn't force this. "I said, *let go*."

When he didn't, I twisted, driving an elbow into his stomach as I attempted to hop over the trunk and back into the center of the room. His grip loosened for a moment, but he didn't quite release me; instead, he twisted my arm behind my back so that I fell, barely avoiding hitting my head against the corner of the trunk when my knees struck the ground.

Before I recovered, he pulled me to my feet and then shoved me toward the mound of blankets piled on the bed.

Furious and frightened at the same time, I managed to lash out once more, striking him in the chest with the heel of my boot. He doubled over, spitting out a string of curses in his own language that I never wanted to have translated.

I hurried back into the cold night before he could follow. I would just have to hope I was well enough to get by. I couldn't risk staying at the mercy of Velyo Frektane. One or the other of us wasn't likely to survive it.

"Oliza?"

I hesitated when I heard Pratl's voice. "I have to leave," I said quickly. "Thank you for your hospitality, and please thank Ginna."

He glanced toward the cabin I had just fled, and winced. Then he drew a knife, and for a moment I thought he meant to stop me. Instead, he offered it to me, handle first. "Just to help you hunt on your way. Don't use it on him." He looked again toward the doorway as I took the weapon. "Go. I'll try to delay him if he comes after you."

"Thank you," I whispered.

"You should not travel long alone," Pratl warned. "You are not well."

"I don't think I have a choice."

He nodded reluctantly. "Go. Be well."

I ran, for the moment concerned more with removing myself from Frektane land than with choosing a destination.

Only after I was back in the woods did shapeshifting occur to me, and then I remembered that I did not have my wings.

Three weeks to Wyvern's Court, Pratl had said; it would

be more than three weeks if I had to travel alone without supplies through unfamiliar land. I knew that Wyvern's Court had to be south from here, but I had never made such a trek by myself.

I tried desperately to take my wyvern form but again felt only a queasy rolling in my stomach. Desperate to reassure myself, I reached for my cobra form—and found nothing. *Nothing.*

The poison lingers. Dear sky, I hope it won't linger forever. I knew that a similar poison was used by the dancers' guild when a punishment required someone to be held in one form for some time, but that wore off in a few days at most. I hoped this would be the same. I had lost my avian form; I could not lose my cobra, too.

Had the lions stolen the poison while in Wyvern's Court? I wondered. Or had their employer given it to them? They might even have had it already.

South, Oliza, my scattered wits reminded me. *You don't have the information you need to find answers, and you won't have any more information until you get home. Your people need you. You've no choice but to walk, so walk.* My fury at Velyo and at my situation in general kept me warm, and I made good time as I jogged and walked south through the night.

It was nearly sunrise when I grudgingly accepted that I needed to sleep. I wished I could make a fire, but my hands were shaking and I could barely keep my eyes open; the idea of searching for dry wood and struggling to make a spark was overwhelming. Fortunately, this night was not as bitter as the one before, and I was able to find shelter in a warm nook where a pine had been knocked down across a boulder.

I curled up inside, my stomach rumbling. I would need

to figure out how to find food and make a fire later. But for now, sleep.

I woke near noon to find a furry gray-brown ball at the entrance to my little den. It lifted its muzzle and licked me when I blinked at it in confusion.

"Morning, Betia," I greeted with a smile of relief. "Thank you for finding me and guarding my rest."

The wolf yawned, stretched, shook herself and let out a little bark. Then she plodded to a large deer that she had obviously taken down earlier and saved for me.

"Thank you," I said. *And thank you, too, Pratl, for the knife,* I thought as I clumsily butchered the deer. The tree I had slept under provided dry wood, so I managed to cook as much of the meat as we could consume right then.

Betia watched me with an intelligence and patience that said she knew what I was doing. I spoke to her as I worked, and while she didn't respond, I had a feeling she understood much of what I said, too.

"I can understand why you ran away," I confided when we began to walk again. The afternoon was bitter, but at least it wasn't snowing. "I couldn't stand Velyo, either."

Betia growled beside me, and I laughed a little.

"I think that's a good way to put it."

She growled again, and as I turned, I realized she was looking into the trees. I did not have a wolf's sense of smell or hearing, but I could hear . . . something.

Something unfriendly, by the sound of Betia's growling. Someone shouted deeper in the woods, and I recognized the voice of one of the lions.

I looked at Betia, my heart racing, and then we ran, slipping through the trees, stumbling over downed logs and brush. In their lion forms, my hunters were much faster than I was; I wished again that I could shift.

We were going to be overtaken, and I didn't stand a chance with just my knife against the claws of a pride of lions. Even if Betia helped me, she was only one, and I knew there were at least a half dozen of them.

"Oliza!" Tavisan's voice floated through the trees. "Stop running!"

He had broken a bone in my wing, clipped my feathers, drugged and poisoned me; I wasn't anxious to talk about it.

Suddenly Betia and I were tumbling down a bank I had not noticed. Betia let out a yelp, and then I was back on flat ground, the air knocked out of my lungs. The wolf nosed my rib cage, encouraging me to get back up; bracing myself on her shoulders, I dragged myself up again.

Luckily, our pursuers were delayed by the drop-off. Maybe they weren't being paid enough to risk broken necks—but who could have hired them to go this far? They knew who I was. What payment could possibly make it worthwhile for them to risk both the serpiente and avian armies' coming after them?

I didn't know how long Betia and I had run, using stream banks to obscure our footsteps and distort our scent, sleeping for only a few minutes at a time before my pounding heart woke me again.

Two sunrises, three sunrises. The world began to waver under me and finally I forced myself to slow our pace. I did not know how near the lions were, but I knew I couldn't go on that way.

With someone after us, I knew better than to go due

south as I had planned. Betia and I varied our direction; I mostly followed as she led us to streams with fish, rabbit burrows, brooks with fresh water and sheltered spots where sleep was easy to find.

Evenings, I lay awake in whatever hollow we had chosen for a bed that night, shivering from chills caused by more than the winter air. I kept food in my stomach through sheer force of will, fighting the twists in my gut because I knew I needed the energy the food provided. I needed my strength. I needed to make it home.

CHAPTER 11

I didn't know how long we had been traveling—a fortnight, maybe—when the day turned black without warning. I fell to my knees and heard Betia's frantic bark. Despite my best efforts, when I tried to push myself up, I couldn't find the strength. I was dizzy and sick from poisons and too many days of running.

Betia whimpered and nuzzled my shoulder, but my abused body had had enough. My stomach cramped as a bout of heavy coughing made me curl into a little ball on the cold ground. I coughed until I gagged, and even afterward I couldn't keep my body from shaking.

The wolf was running in desperate circles around me, barking every now and then to encourage me.

She disappeared, and I was overwhelmed by another coughing fit. I had to stand up; we had to keep moving.

I had pushed myself to my knees by the time Betia returned, her coat dripping wet and her brown eyes apologetic. She must have run back to the river, to try to bring me something to eat.

I lifted a hand and put it on her shoulder. She licked fever sweat from my cheek, and I closed my eyes.

I was on the ground again, and I was sick, and I was cold, and I was lost, and I was frightened. Betia was frightened, too, and I wanted to say something to comfort her, but I could think of nothing.

What was happening in my home while I was lying there? What had happened with the dancers? With the Vahamil? For all I knew, I might return to a war.

Suddenly hands were on my shoulders and someone was lifting me into a sitting position. For an instant I thought the mercenaries had found me, but I couldn't summon terror. I felt only protected. Gentle fingers brushed my cheek, and then someone was holding a cup of cool, sweet water to my lips. I realized then how tight and raw my throat was from coughing. I tried to stand again, but strong arms held me still. When I shivered, they held me more tightly.

Night fell, and those arms kept me warm in the darkness. When I woke, I was offered more water. As if by magic, a fire had appeared. When I woke again, sometime after sunrise, it was to the scent of cooking meat. I ate a little, though my appetite was still poor, and drank more water; then I slept once again.

It was another day before the fever broke, and I opened my eyes and finally looked with clear vision upon the woman who had cared for me.

Her thick hair was light brown, with darker, ruddy shades. Her skin was tanned, and her arms and face had streaks of dirt. Her eyes were a familiar, warm brown, with dark, heavy lashes.

"Good morning, Betia," I said.

She looked at me and yawned and stretched, just as she had the first morning. She did not speak aloud, and I didn't know if she even remembered how. Speech was one thing that most shapeshifters who went feral never recovered. Still, that she had been able to recall her human body was a good sign. Her concern for me and her need for a form more suited to caring for me must have driven her back from her wolf.

She put a hand to my brow to check my fever.

"You keep taking care of me," I remarked as she turned to tend the last flickers of the fire with easy skill.

Betia glanced back at me and tilted her head the way a natural wolf would have when puzzled. I wondered what thoughts were passing behind those earthen eyes. She smiled and then returned to the rabbit she had set to cook over the low-burning embers. Had she caught it before she'd returned to human form, or was she still an excellent huntress even without a wolf's speed, strength or ferocity?

Of course she was, I decided. The Frektane tribe belonged only to those who could take care of themselves and their pack—and Velyo would never have been interested in a weak woman with nothing to offer him.

The thought gave me a chill that had nothing to do with my illness. I realized for the first time that Betia was dressed in simple pants made from soft wool and a loose blouse of the same material, with fluffy sleeves and an airy fit. Her feet were bare, and her hair was down around her face in tangled waves.

Dressed like that, she had probably been alone in her

own room, relaxing or perhaps preparing to sleep, before she had taken her wolf form and run from her people. Alone—or with someone she had trusted.

By the next day we had started moving again, more slowly this time. Each day took us farther south, though we kept an ear out for signs of pursuit.

If I had worried about Betia's ability to travel in human form, I had been wrong to. Not even bare feet seemed to bother her, though I was glad we were no longer in the snow. She ran ahead occasionally, slipping through the trees like a sprite but always returning before peaceful solitude turned to loneliness.

I saw my reflection in a pool where we stopped for water, and I grimaced. I was beyond lean—thin, dangerously so. The drugs should have worn off weeks before, but I hadn't had enough food or rest, and my body simply didn't have the resources to fight the poison. I could still feel it in my blood, and with every step, I knew that I risked bringing the fever back. I simply didn't have any choice.

I was lucky to have Betia with me. She had a knack for finding drinking water, as well as caches of nuts hidden by squirrels. She also could tickle fish from the streams, seeming not to care about water or mud—and I had not forgotten that she had somehow caught that rabbit, alone and unarmed.

I still did not know what had possessed her to follow me, or to save me in the first place. I wondered if I was doing her a disservice by taking her with me. She obviously did not want to return to the Frektane, but was Wyvern's Court, in its state of distrust and turmoil, really a place where she could be happy?

More and more I wished I could join her in the forest, as serene and natural as she seemed to be.

"Your brother, Pratl, was the one who told me your name," I said to her in the midst of one of our many one-sided conversations. "He cares for you a great deal, it seems."

She tensed beside me, her step faltering, and did not even look my way.

"Your mother also seems to be a kind woman." I described the odd morning when I had met both Pratl and Ginna, not moving on to discuss the rest of the day. I knew that Betia didn't want to hear anything about the leaders of her pack.

"They must love you," I mused aloud, thinking of my own loved ones. My parents—not to mention the rest of my family, and most of the court—would be frantic with worry over my disappearance.

Everyone would be, except whoever had paid to have me removed. . . .

"I know you were hurt, and you're frightened, but couldn't you still go back—"

Betia shot me a look that clearly said, *Do not speak of that.*

"Betia . . ."

She dropped her gaze for an instant, then looked at me with a plea in her eyes, reaching out to touch my arm.

"I didn't mean to upset you," I said. "I was just thinking about the people from my home, who I love, and who I miss, and who must be so frightened for me. If you never want to return to the Frektane, that is your choice. If you want to come to Wyvern's Court, you can have a new life there, or if you want to be with other wolves, Kalisa's pack would probably take you in." Unless, of course, Kalisa was no longer in charge of the Vahamil when I returned.

Kalisa, injured. The dancers, demanding answers. Wyvern's Court, torn by violence.

And me, wandering around in the endless woods.

I let out a frustrated cry, and Betia leaned against my side and put her arms around me.

The mercenaries never should have been able to take me from Wyvern's Court. They never should have been able to take me through forests patrolled by my guards and occupied by the Vahamil.

They never should have *wanted* to. Who could convince the lions to risk the wrath of a realm such as Wyvern's Court? We were a peaceful nation, but we had warred for many years; the death toll on both sides showed just how skillful my people had been at killing each other. It would take a lot to force Wyvern's Court to turn back to war, but kidnapping the heir to both thrones was a good start.

Or was that the point?

Someone wanted me not just removed but transported a great distance. Someone had gone to great trouble and great expense to meet that goal. Someone . . . was behind me.

I froze, then moved only my arm to reach toward my knife. Why hadn't I heard them approach?

Betia snarled, and bush branches snapped as she pounced. I spun toward the interlopers, raising the knife, evading one attack.

Serpiente—at least three of them in my immediate view. The real criminals?

No time to wonder, my mind snapped. *Defend yourself first.*

Betia and I moved back to back as if we had rehearsed it. "Three on my side," I said aloud, though I didn't expect a response from her. A quick glance revealed another two on hers. The serpiente in front of me had the palest blond hair I had ever seen, and light blue-green eyes.

Two against five. Not good odds, especially since the serpents wore two knives crossed on their backs, and three of them were also armed with strong wooden staves tipped with blades that gleamed wickedly in the sunlight. One wore a bow in addition to this.

"Drop the knife," the man in front of me said.

I didn't have a choice, really. Fighting now would probably get me killed. If these were the people who had had me abducted in the first place, they wanted me alive, and dropping the knife would be the better option.

Before I could act, Betia snarled and someone behind me cried out. Seizing the moment of surprise, I leapt for a man holding a stave; I knew how to use it. I hit him in the gut, knocking us both to the ground, and reached for the weapon with my free hand.

We rolled, and I came up with the stave, which I tried to snap down across my enemy's head. He blocked, rolling enough to deflect most of the blow, then came up with a snarl. White scales coated his skin, and his eyes became pure blue except for slit pupils. Snake eyes, in his fighting form. I wished I could summon my own, with its increased speed, flexibility and reflexes, as well as enough poison to make any enemy hesitate.

I rolled away, swinging the stave; I felt it strike one of the other attackers across the ribs.

Someone pounced on me from behind; an arm wrapped around my throat, and I turned the knife in my hand to drive it backward. I felt it hit something, but then my wrist was grabbed and the knife was wrenched from my hand. An elbow to my attacker got me dislodged and tossed into an inelegant heap on the ground, nearly at the feet of a woman.

She gripped the front of my shirt, then froze and let out a piercing whistle.

Startled, she half hissed, half shouted, "Peace! Weapons *down*." There was an *oomph* as someone behind me was hit, and the woman said to me, "Call off your friend." She stood, dropping her stave. "I didn't realize who you were."

"Betia, stop!" They had us outnumbered and out-armed. There was no reason for them to let us go unless the woman was being honest. Looking around, I saw that we had done a surprising amount of damage, but I had no doubt that we would have lost eventually.

Betia was still in her human form, thank the sky; if she had returned to her wolf to fight, I would have worried that she might not come back again.

The woman who had pinned me offered me a hand, saying, *"Fm'itil-varl'nesera."*

Shocked, I took a moment to translate the words. You bless us, dancer. My hand went to the coin at my neck, the *Ahnleh* my mother had passed on to me, and I gave the traditional reply. *"Fm'varl'nesera-hena."* Blessed be.

CHAPTER 12

My heart was still pounding, even though the fight was over. I had been formally greeted as a traveling dancer, based on an archaic law that almost no one remembered these days.

"I apologize," my former opponent said. "Normally we do not tolerate strangers in our lands, but anyone with a Snakecharm is welcome here, and safe—as in days before. I am sorry I did not see it sooner."

"And my friend?" I asked. "She is not a dancer."

"If she is your friend, she is ours."

I brushed myself off and went to Betia's side unchallenged. I had not known there was any place left that still honored such old traditions, but as it seemed to be working in my favor, I would not argue.

"Betia, are you all right?" I asked.

A man knelt beside us. "She's bleeding," he said. "Come, let us care for her wounds—yours as well, dancer. And our own," he added wryly. I realized he was the one whose skull I had tried to knock in with a stave. "You fight well, especially considering that you look half-starved and exhausted. We will see to your injuries; then you will eat and rest here."

Their generosity forced me to be honest. "I am being hunted. And I am not really a dancer. I have learned some, from Wyvern's Nest, but I am not even officially apprenticed."

He smiled anyway. "Someone thought you worthy of wearing the *Ahnleh*. So you are welcome. As for your hunters . . ." The smiled changed to a hungry one. "You are among the Obsidian tribe. We have more than steel to keep you safe, if need be."

"Are you the leader here?" I asked tentatively. Perhaps I was not so safe. The Obsidian guild was a group of outlaws. The nearly colorless hair and eyes of some, if not their ivory scales, should have told me. White vipers, Maeve's descendants, they had lived as outsiders since their ancestors had been driven away for practicing dark magic that endangered the serpiente. They had defied Cobriana rule for millennia, occasionally joined by other serpents who had either chosen to leave serpiente society or been exiled for crimes.

"Perhaps," he answered, with a teasing smile. "Perhaps not. You are looking at me as if I have sprouted wings— though for you, that might not be strange." He tickled the back of my neck, ruffling the feathers there and making me jump. His expression turned serious. "I know who you are, Oliza Shardae Cobriana, princess of Wyvern's Court. I recognized you as soon as I saw you. But you still wear the charm. That grants you safety, a meal and a bed, no matter whose blood you carry or who travels with you."

My whole body sagged with fatigue and relief. "Thank you. Your generosity will not be ignored."

He laughed. "Oh, ignore it, please. We've no desire to join your court. Certainly no desire to come to the attention of your parents. You may stay as long as you like and leave whenever you like, but once you are gone, I hope you will forget us entirely. Now, please, join us for supper, *fm'itil* and *tair'feng,* dancer and wolf."

Our wounds were tended, as were those we had delivered; no one seemed to hold a grudge about the injuries, though Betia delivered more than one amused look my way. She sat beside me while we ate. Although they were friendly, no one introduced herself or himself by name; I noticed that the names they used for each other shifted from one moment to the next.

"So tell us, dancer; you said you're not even apprenticed, but you would not be wearing a Snakecharm if you did not know something?" one said as the night wore on.

"I cannot officially be apprenticed to the nest because of my position in Wyvern's Court," I answered. People nodded; it seemed everyone here knew who I was. "However, I have learned as much as my nest's leader will teach me."

"What steps do you know?"

I sighed, considering. "Blade dances are my favorites," I answered, "but I love everything. I know about fifteen of the *sakkri,* and most of the *she'da.* Of course I have learned the *Namir-da,* though I have never performed it, and I know the four *harja* types and six of the thirteen formal *melos* variations, though I have never danced them outside of my teacher's class, either."

"How old are you?" someone asked bluntly.

"Twenty." I knew what the next question would be. "It's my own choice not to perform the *rrasatoth* dances." The *rrasatoth* dances included the *melos* and the *harja,* as well as certain pieces such as the *Namir-da.* That reminded me of

Urban's teasing offer to dance with me at Salem's reception. I wished my last memories of him could have been that light.

The man I had first spoken to, a white viper I suspected was the leader despite his refusal to admit it, said firmly, "Then we'll respect that choice. Though if tomorrow you are feeling well enough, perhaps we might see something you enjoy."

Dinner ended when I was just reaching the sleepy haze that follows an excellent meal. Betia and I were offered a bed in one of the few shelters. It was a beautiful night for sleeping outside, but our host pointed out that it would be best if Betia and I were not seen by anyone who passed by—namely the mercenaries who had been following us.

I spoke to Betia as we drifted into sleep—about dances, about the beautiful *melos* and about how I wished I could dance those steps without all the hassle that came with them. I told her of the *Ahnleh* and how it had come to me, and then of the history of the Obsidian guild, from the genesis of the serpiente to the modern-day position of Maeve's kin.

Betia leaned against me, snuggling closer, and I took it as encouragement to continue.

"The white vipers have never acknowledged a Cobriana as their king," I finished. "Some of my ancestors have tried to force them, and some have tried to make peace with them, but the guild stays as it has always been—a group of drifters. The white vipers are the heart of the guild, though sometimes other serpents join them." I did not explain that these were usually former soldiers who had been branded traitors for refusing to fight during war times. Criminals who were no longer accepted by their own families and friends also went into the woods sometimes. Supposedly, justice among the guild was harsh enough that these criminals were forced to reform or else were kicked out of their last possible haven.

Betia yawned beside me, and soon we both fell asleep. I felt safe and warm for the first time since I had found Urban unconscious on the cold cobbles of the northern hills.

CHAPTER 13

The Obsidian guild implored me to stay for a few days to recover my strength before traveling, and as eager as I was to get back to Wyvern's Court, I knew they were right.

Betia bounced back to perfect health like a puppy, and soon she was laughing and occasionally humming a melody I did not know. Though she remained in human form, she still had a tendency to pounce like a young wolf at play, sending us tumbling across the soft ground until we were covered in dirt and leaves but laughing too hard to stand up. Despite the horror that had led to this situation, and despite my fears of what I would find when I reached home, I was thankful to have this time. I had never had a friend who was completely unaffected by my status in Wyvern's Court. It was nice to be a person instead of a title.

As a result of the good food, the chance to sleep well and the healthy exercise, gradually I started to feel like myself again. The nightmares that had plagued me did not completely disappear, but I was able to shake them off during the day. My serpent form returned to me, which left me both relieved and heartsick.

I could not imagine returning to Wyvern's Court without my wings. I could not imagine facing pity from the avians, or horror from those who would now consider me even more a serpent. I could not imagine facing the ignorance of my serpiente friends, who would never comprehend what I had lost.

But it was time. I had no place in this world if it wasn't in Wyvern's Court.

On the last day we planned to spend with the guild, Betia left early in the morning to hunt with some of Obsidian's people, and I remained behind, speaking with their leader. When the white viper pointed out that the winter solstice was only a couple of weeks away, I was reminded of how fast time was flying.

We would be leaving the next day. I would be home in time for the Namir-da holiday, which celebrated the birth of the serpiente people. Thinking of it made me wonder about the group I was currently with. "Tell me of your people," I said finally. "I know the stories as they have been told by my ancestors, but I would like to hear how you tell them."

He hesitated, his eyes searching the skies, and then agreed. "Long ago, there were thirteen high priests and priestesses, known as the Dasi, who were led by Maeve; there were also two groups, the Nesera'rsh and the Ealla'rsh, who were lesser priests and priestesses. Maeve and the Dasi spoke to the gods. They brought the rain, and peace and prosperity for their people. The Rsh spoke to the villagers. They made sure everyone was heard and no one was forgotten. They were the healers and judges, and they taught the common people the worship of *Ahnleh*. They answered to no one and nothing but Fate herself.

"They believed," he explained, "that every soul was connected to every other, and therefore that none was better than any other. They believed that each person was a part of the whole and led and followed as Fate decreed—and that the position of each person shifted through his life. They kept their true names between themselves and the gods, because in the wider world, we are all anonymous. When we call another person by name, it is just another name for ourselves.

"Of course you know the story told in the *Namir-da,* of how Maeve seduced Leben in order to protect her people, and he gave to her the second form of a white viper, and to the rest of her people serpent and falcon forms." He paused and finally said, "That is the entire story that the Cobriana tell. What they do not mention is that Maeve had a lover before Leben. They do not tell that part of the tale because that lover was one of the Dasi—Kiesha, the high priestess of Anhamirak."

My eyes widened. Kiesha had been the first cobra.

"Kiesha was devastated by what she thought was Maeve's betrayal. Even after Leben was gone, she refused to forgive Maeve. Instead, she took a mate and bore to him a son she named Diente. You know the rest of that story, because Diente was the first king of your line. As for our line . . ."

"Our myths say that Maeve started practicing black magic," I said when the silence grew long.

"Ahnmik, the dark god who is Anhamirak's opposite, grants the numb peace sought by a man or woman whose love has turned elsewhere. He whispers promises of rest and of release from pain, and Maeve succumbed to those lures. So Kiesha's people drove her away."

"And then?"

"The Nesera'rsh took her in. Gradually, she withdrew from Ahnmik's numbness, accepting life once again. She took a mate. Her descendants are the white vipers of today. We follow the ways of the Nesera'rsh, as well as we can."

"Two generations ago, Maeve's kin were pardoned by the Cobriana," I said, broaching the subject tentatively. "The Obsidian guild was invited to join the rest of the serpiente. Only two white vipers came. I know your people have been treated poorly in the past, but surely the time has come when you no longer need to live like outlaws."

"Wyvern's Court is already struggling to bridge one ancient rift. Now is not the time to fight to close another," he pointed out. "Besides, my people would only follow someone who they knew understood and respected their ways. The Cobriana have not earned that trust; the Shardae line of hawks certainly has not."

"I wasn't asking you to kneel to me," I said, hoping I had not given that impression. "I was just offering you a place to call home. As long as you didn't break any of our laws, no one would demand obeisance."

"You have had ancestors who promised pardons and delivered mass executions," he pointed out. "Others have invited us to their land only to decide after a few years that we were not respectful enough. It did not help that one of the two vipers who went to serpiente lands was executed shortly after. I'm inclined to believe your father's word that Adelina was guilty of treason, but my kin have learned not to be too trusting."

"Yet you took me in."

"You wear the *Ahnleh*," he said, as if that was all that mattered. Maybe it was. "And I might have wanted to meet the wyvern who would be queen of this impossible realm. I do not trust easily, but that does not mean I have no hope for the future. When I was a young child, your uncle used to walk these woods. Anjay Cobriana would spend nights here sometimes, when he could get away from his guards. He would dance with us, and for a while we could forget that by blood we were enemies. If he had lived, we might have followed him. But that *if* speaks of the past. Now I speak to the child of Anjay's younger brother, Oliza Shardae Cobriana, who has more pressing issues at the moment than my people."

Before more could be said, Betia and the others returned. Obviously impressed, her companions informed me that Betia could gather fish from the river as if her hands were made of netting. The mute wolf smiled proudly, holding up her catch.

During dinner we made light conversation that turned deeper when one of the pythons of the guild sighed. "It's a pity you don't perform the *rrasatoth* dances," she said.

I shrugged a little, though I knew it did not hide my regret. "It's a decision I've made. I don't want to be pressured—"

"That's what's so unfair," the python interrupted. "If you were forty years old and had been performing *rrasatoth* since you were sixteen, all you would need to tell a suitor is that you aren't interested. You shouldn't be denied the dances just because you aren't ready to choose a partner."

"I would think a child of Obsidian wouldn't have such a passionate belief in fairness, considering how you have been treated in the past."

She gave a shrug that conveyed the same things that mine had earlier: acknowledgement and regret. "A dancer who cannot dance because her nestmates won't respect her desire *not* to choose a lover is just as confined as an avian lady who is ostracized because she chooses to have one. That isn't freedom. Perhaps it is no wonder your people have forgotten Anhamirak's magic, if they have so obviously forgotten her lessons."

Some sense of tension I got from her made me turn to Betia then. Betia's beautiful brown eyes dropped when I focused on her, but then she smiled. So I didn't understand why she stood up and walked inside.

I wanted to follow her, but my companion caught my wrist. "She'll be back. I think I know what she's after. She was working on it earlier."

Betia returned then and placed a soft bundle that felt like silk in my hands. The material slid across my fingers, and I caught my breath as I opened it.

The *melos* was simple, a single piece of cream-colored silk with an uncomplicated boarder stitched in golden thread. There were no tassels, no chimes, no fringes or complicated patterns—and I knew that it would always be my most cherished possession.

"Dance," the python said. "No one here is going to tell Wyvern's Court that we saw Oliza Shardae Cobriana dancing a *melos*. No one would believe us anyway."

I pulled Betia into a hug. She knew exactly what this meant to me. She didn't have to speak it aloud: *Dance.*

When was the last time I had let myself feel joy without reserve? I couldn't recall. This would be one of those times.

I stepped onto the dais. I knew the variation I would perform: *hanlah'melos.* And I knew who I would be performing for. I looked into the wolf's eyes and heard the music begin.

I felt as if I moved in a sphere of fire and electricity, and anything I touched would meet that charge.

Why had I refused this feeling before? In that moment, I

believed with all my soul that any trouble it might bring was more than worth it. I could survive with nothing else if I could just dance and have someone to dance for.

At the end, I stepped off the dais and knew that every eye in the camp—far more than those of the four people who had been watching at the start—was on me.

I saw only one person.

I hooked the scarf across Betia's shoulders and grasped her hands as if I could channel into her this incredible feeling of possibility. Maybe I did.

We both jumped when a viper, one of the two professional-level dancers who traveled with the Obsidian guild, stepped toward us.

"For someone who has never performed publicly, you were amazing. Actually, that was amazing even if you had been dancing for years. Something to be said for cross-breeding," she said, joking. "I would love to share the dais with you someday."

"Thank you," I said, snapping out of my trance. Betia's hand was still twined with my left one, and I gave her an apologetic smile. She shrugged off the interruption, giving me a friendly shove toward the other dancer.

The serpent laughed. "I think that was an order to do so now. Do you know the *san'asi*?"

Literally, the name meant *raising the gods*; it was one of the most exotic of the *sakkri*, and Urban, Salem and I had performed it together on more than one occasion.

"I know it," I answered.

The viper offered her hand, inviting me to join her and her companion, a man who had amused Betia and me the past several nights with stories and songs.

The *san'asi* was one of the more complicated versions of

the dance. I knew it well, but my ability to perform would be entirely dependent on how well I could sense and predict my partners' movements and work seamlessly with them. I didn't want to make a fool out of myself.

I took the white viper's hand, then glanced at Betia, who was seated in front of the dais, watching me and waiting. She flashed a challenging smile, the glint in her eyes daring.

The three of us must have been quite a sight, all balanced effortlessly on the balls of our feet, forearms crossed before us, facing each other in a triangle so that our fingertips just touched: white viper, Burmese python, and me.

If only Wyvern's Court could achieve this. One little symbol, the *Ahnleh* my mother had given to me, had allowed me to join this mixed group. If only I could forge such a powerful talisman for my home.

CHAPTER 14

One of the Obsidian guild played the flute, the simple instrument that had always been the main accompaniment to the serpents' dances.

Breath attuned, heartbeats in sync, we moved into the ancient dance. There was nothing else beyond the dais.

As the three of us moved, the air seemed to ripple. It was as if we were alone, two spirits in three bodies. The pressure grew, and abruptly I realized that something was *wrong—*

Two? It should have been three, or one. I knew where the white viper was when I danced, but the python was a foreign entity.

I wasn't the only one who stumbled. Nothing touched us, but I found myself fighting off tremors. I pushed myself up and saw the white viper kneeling by the third dancer's side.

The guild's leader spoke behind me. "Kiesha's line hasn't demonstrated any talent with the old coven's magic since Maeve was driven away," he said, his voice holding something that sounded like awe. "I didn't imagine you would be the first, Wyvern."

"I don't have magic," I answered. My throat was dry. What had happened? I felt much the way I had when Hai's power had overwhelmed me before I spoke to Marus and Prentice.

Betia put a hand on my arm, questioning.

"I'm all right," I said softly. "It was . . ." Already the sensations were fading. I felt as if, for a moment, I had touched something incredible, but then it was gone.

The white viper came to my side, her face glowing with admiration. "That—" She laughed. "I've read descriptions, of course, that say a true *sakkri* is too powerful even to be recalled by the mind without practice. But I never imagined—"

She stopped when she saw the confused expression on my face. "*Sakkri.* These days they're just a type of dance, but once they were powerful spells. No serpent has been able to spin one since Maeve's time. And even if we could, I understand that the mind can't see them or make sense of them without training. They fade away like dreams."

That was certainly one way to describe this lingering feeling; it was as if I had woken abruptly, just as my mind had reached for sleep and the land of dreams. Was this what Hai had tried to explain to me? *The mind barely comprehends its own yesterday, but* sakkri *force on it other times, other places, other people, visions it tries to shake away because to hold them all would only court madness.*

"You seem much less confused by this than I am," I said, trying to make sense of what had happened.

"A white viper is no stranger to magic. We never lost ours the way Kiesha's kin did. But Maeve's position in the Dasi was as one who preserved *balance*, not as one who worked the higher magics," the white viper explained patiently. "Even in the early days, we never possessed the sheer power that could be woven by Kiesha or Cjarsa."

Never in all my days in Wyvern's Court would a serpent have casually said the name of the first cobra and the name of the falcon Empress in the same breath. Hearing them together now, in this context, made me feel a little lost. On the other hand, the connection did make me remember something Nicias had said.

"A falcon once explained to me that their magic is disturbed by what is left of the magic the Cobriana once had. The remnants act like a spark. Maybe it does the same with yours."

One of the other vipers nodded thoughtfully. "That's probably all it was, then. After all, it isn't often that a cobra dances with a white viper. It seems to have taken a toll on you, though. Maybe you should lie down for a few minutes."

"Yes. Yes, I think I will."

Betia and I returned to the tent that had been set aside for our use. "I'm . . . all right," I assured Betia, who was watching me with a worried expression. "I don't think wyverns are cut out for magic." I briefly described the unpleasant incident with Hai that had occurred while we were trying to deal with Urban.

He would be walking again by now, I realized. I leaned against Betia with a sigh. "I wish there *was* some magic that would let me know what was going on at home. Being here, dancing, almost makes me forget how scared I am of what might be happening while I'm gone, but then it all comes flooding back."

The tent flap opened just enough to allow one of the Obsidian guild vipers to slither inside. The serpent returned to human form to explain swiftly, "Intruders, lions. They look like they might be the mercenaries who have been after you. We can deal with them, as long as they don't know you're here, so stay quiet for a little while, all right?"

We nodded, and she left the same way she had come, discreetly in case anyone was watching the camp.

It wasn't long before we heard loud voices outside. It sounded as if the Obsidian guild was inviting the mercenaries to join them for supper.

"We're looking for a pair of thieves," the lions' leader said. "Two girls—a wolf and a bird. One has dark hair, gold eyes, real distinctive."

There were some questioning murmurs as the Obsidian guild consulted its own people.

"No thieves here," someone answered. I had to bite my hand to keep from laughing. The Obsidian guild, while friendly to a traveling dancer, was generally considered a group of outlaws.

"You sure? Mind if we look around?"

I held my breath until I heard an indignant, "Yes, we mind. We offer you hospitality, and you offer mistrust in return. Sit!" It wasn't an invitation. "Maybe if you join us for a spell, we might be more inclined to believe you're friendly. Especially if you have something to trade for the information."

The mercenaries mumbled an apology. I gathered that they agreed to join the guild for a meal.

"I know you aren't looking for thieves," I heard someone say a bit later. "You're mercenaries; you've passed through here before. Who are you working for now?"

"Can't tell that," one of the lions answered gruffly.

"Honestly, you must know," the serpent said, pushing.

"*I* know; my men do not," the leader said before anyone else could speak. "And it is not information I am at liberty to give out, no matter how . . . grateful . . . I am for your . . . hospitality." There was an odd hesitation in his response, as if he was having trouble speaking.

"Someone must want these two pretty badly," a serpent observed.

"Yes" was the only reply.

A while later everything was quiet. Betia and I waited until our host stepped into the hut with a smirk and a chuckle. "I hate rude people."

"Where—"

"Drugged," he answered simply. "Sleeping off some of their own poisons, from their own bags, which my people have lightened just a little. There's no reference in the leader's bags about who hired him, but we did find this. I believe it's yours." He held out a sheathed dagger that I instantly recognized as one my mother had passed on to me. It had been given to her on the day the last avian-serpiente battle had been fought, and it had never once been drawn. She had handed it to me with the prayer *I hope you need it as often as I have.*

"It is." I tied the dagger to my belt to keep it safe. "Why would the lions have had it?"

He quirked one brow and admitted, "Probably for the same reason that one of my people took it. It's very well made, a work of art in addition to being a weapon, and therefore valuable. If the lions found it while they were looking for you, I imagine they didn't hesitate in taking it. And they're going to be cross when they wake up and find it gone. We can defend ourselves without any problem, but I would rather you and Betia weren't caught in the middle of it. I think it's time the two of you moved on."

It had been one of the most amazing days of my life. I had the *melos* that Betia had given me tied at my waist, and all I needed to do was touch it to break out in a grin. But all good things must end.

I had another life to return to, one with responsibilities and expectations. I reached for Betia's hand as I stepped out of the hut, and tried to remember the optimism and faith that she had brought out in me.

"Thank you, for everything," I said to the members of the Obsidian guild.

Our host shook his head. "Our hospitality was nothing more than the *Ahnleh* should ensure you anywhere. Though if gratitude will keep you from speaking to your parents of us . . . ?"

I nodded. "If you wish to be unknown, it would be a poor reward for me to go against that wish."

"I'll send a couple of my people with you, to guide you until you meet up with the Vahamil. They should be able to take you the rest of the way to Wyvern's Court."

"*Teska.*" Thank you.

The leader of the Obsidian guild smiled. "*A'le-Ahnleh-itil.* If ever I would acknowledge a queen, perhaps it would be you. But that time isn't here yet. *Wimashe.*"

"*Wimashe-lalintoth.*" Goodbye, friend.

CHAPTER 15

We reached Vahamil land sooner than I'd expected. Betia scented wolves before I had a chance to warn her, and she went rigid, recoiling. I had just turned to encourage her when a familiar male voice shouted my name. At the sound, Betia whimpered, turned on her heel and ran. *Velyo.* I turned to go after Betia but stopped when I felt pressure on my arm, a hand restraining me from running. I shook off Velyo's grip, but Betia had too much of a head start, and a wolf running in fear would always be faster than the human who followed her.

Surrounded by unfamiliar woods, I shouted, "Betia, please! You're safe with me; you know you're always safe with me—"

"Oliza?" Velyo said again, drawing my attention back to him.

Furious, I spun about. The other wolves that had been around us backed off, including some that I recognized from the Vahamil pack.

Right now I wasn't interested in them—only the man I had hoped never to see again. "What kind of leader *are* you?"

I demanded, shaking with rage. "She runs from you in *terror*. What did you do to her—or do I have to ask?"

I shoved past him, remembering the last scene between us. He refused to move, and my shoulder caught him in the chest, knocking him back.

Betia would never come to me, not while he was there. "What are you doing here, anyway?" I snapped as he walked after me. "Following me?"

"Believe it or not, I do take my responsibilities rather seriously," he replied. "You might not have wanted our help, but I felt that it was important to tell your people what I knew of your situation. While I was here, I wanted to see to my people who winter with the Vahamil, especially since Kalisa isn't certain she will be continuing in her position. Now, if you're done with your tantrum, there are some things you should know."

"My *tantrum*?" I shouted, feeling every inch a coiled serpent preparing to strike. "Your own people are terrified of you, Velyo. Has that occurred to you?"

"They should be," he replied frankly. "I am their leader, and I have control of their lives or deaths. It is a weak leader whose people do not respect him."

"My people *respect* me," I spat. "Respect and fear are not the—"

"Aren't they?" he asked. "And do they?"

I was filled with cold rage, and I spoke the words I knew I should not. "What you tried to do to me—what I suspect you did to Betia—would carry a death sentence in Wyvern's Court. How long do you think you would survive if I told my guard? That is not because they fear me; it is because they care for me."

"How long do you think you would survive if you declared war on my people?" he said. He held out a hand to me, challenging. "We both know that you won't do it. So why don't you play nice and come back to the camp with me? Your people have been looking for you, frantic as a child missing his blanket. They were not happy to learn that you were traveling alone."

"Thank you," I said, hating to acknowledge his help but knowing that he had not been obligated even to tell my people that I was alive. I did not take his hand, though I tried to force myself to appear calm as I walked back to the camp.

I was not so furious about what he had tried to do to me. I despised him, but I had no authority over him. I could not change his world when I was trying to fix my own.

But I hated him for Betia. I had no doubt that he had frightened her into her wolf form, and even as I walked to Kalisa's camp, I was gnawed by the terror that this might have been too much for her. If she fled into her wolf form now, she might never return.

I stroked the *melos* she had given me, which was still tied at my waist. Though the colors were not the vibrant reds, greens and blues traditionally used, any of my people would recognize it for what it was. I thought about hiding it before I ran into any serpiente, so that I wouldn't have to face their questions, but I couldn't. I might have lost Betia already. I would not put away my only remembrance.

The Vahamil camp was quieter than I had ever heard it, and I quickly realized that Velyo was the reason. His own people watched him with fear; Kalisa's watched him with wary disdain. Kalisa herself greeted him with a polite nod as she stood and walked toward me. Her movements were tight, and they betrayed that she was still in some pain, but her expression was one of welcome and relief as she grasped my hands in her own.

"Kalisa, it is so good to see you," I said to the alpha. "I had heard that you were injured."

"It remains to be seen if I will continue as alpha of the Vahamil," Kalisa replied. "Frektane's presence has intimidated many of my challengers—but only because he has hinted that he is interested in the position. Velyo is not someone I would wish as my successor." She glanced at Velyo, who had gone to speak to one of his wolves. "Fortunately, unlike Frektane's, my position rests on a little more than brute strength. My people are far better off, due to our relationship with Wyvern's Court. Your parents' support has been a great help to me during my recovery." She admitted, "Seeing your parents as terrified as they've been since you disappeared has been heartbreaking. I am very glad to see that you are all right and will be back home soon. We are still a couple of days away by land, but it would not be a long flight."

I shook my head. "I can't fly."

"Velyo was right, then, about the drugs? But they will wear off eventually."

I nodded, though I knew that the drugs were no longer holding me in this shape. I had recovered my cobra form when the drugs had worn off; my wings would not be coming back.

"In the meantime," Kalisa said, "I will send one of my fastest wolves to tell your guard where they can find you. Whoever was responsible for taking you away will probably feel threatened by your return. I think it would be best if you wait until your guards are with you before continuing on your way, I wouldn't travel alone through these woods until the villain is found."

It seemed to be sound advice, though if Velyo had offered it, I probably would have refused. "Thank you," I said. "Can you give me any word on what else is going on in Wyvern's Court?"

I worried that other violence might have followed the attack on Urban, such as serpiente retaliating against those who had harmed one of their own—especially while my parents and I were gone.

"We haven't been in the area recently," she answered. "Your guards came here to ask if we had seen you, but we knew nothing until Velyo arrived. I was horrified to learn that you had been taken through our land without our knowledge."

Looking up from his discussion with another wolf, Velyo said to Kalisa, "I may disagree with your belief that it is not necessary to patrol the border you share with Wyvern's Court, but it is hardly the Vahamil's fault that their neighbors can't keep track of their own princess. Especially when all the pack's resources were dedicated to the welfare of its alpha."

Kalisa refrained from responding, and Velyo, apparently bored of the discussion, turned and left us again.

"Two alphas is too many for one camp," Kalisa said softly after he had gone. "Blue-eyes is a little too eager for me to pass on my authority. The Frektane pack has always been ambitious enough to keep the rest of us on guard."

"He treats his own people like dirt," I said, tact leaving me.

Kalisa shook her head. "The northern packs need to be a

little harsher to survive the winter," she said, though the expression in her eyes did not match the tolerance in her voice. "It isn't my place to question how Velyo runs his pack, only how I run mine."

"But you let them winter with you."

"Should I punish the Frektane people because I don't like their leader?" she asked.

"Leader? What about his father?"

"Dead," Kalisa informed me. "Shortly after you left."

"Frektane did not seem that unwell when I saw him," I said, wondering if Velyo had added patricide to his list of crimes since we'd last met.

"This isn't really a conversation for you, Wyvern," Kalisa replied, confirming my suspicions. "Pack business is pack business, not meant for the ears of Wyvern's Court."

I nodded, accepting the dismissal. Unlike among the Obsidian guild, here I would always be Oliza Shardae Cobriana. When Kalisa spoke to me, it was queen to princess, and that was not a relationship that allowed for idle talk.

"Just . . . be careful," I couldn't resist adding.

"I always am."

Time passed differently among the wolves than inside Wyvern's Court. The days were marked only by sunrise and sunset, and the meals by when a hunter returned. The mellow rhythm was a poor match for my anxiety and frustration. As long as I was with the wolves, I knew that Betia would not come back to me. I was the only one she seemed to trust. And as long as I was away from Wyvern's Court, I would not be able to eat or sleep without the queasy feeling that my world might be crumbling.

CHAPTER 16

A flurry of wings woke me early on my third morning with the wolves. I opened my eyes to see the descent of ten avians, including a peregrine falcon and a golden hawk. I was desperate to see my own people again, and I hurried to meet them.

With a falcon's ability to dive swiftly and gracefully, Nicias landed and returned to human form first. He practically lifted me off the ground as he hugged me with truly serpiente abandon. I noticed a couple of avians averting their gazes as they landed around us, but I tried to ignore them. Birds would forever look away at displays of affection, just as serpents would forever indulge in them. Some things would never change.

Someone behind Nicias cleared her throat, and he sprang away from me to give her room. The other avians—a half dozen from my mother's Royal Flight, and the rest from among my Wyverns—also stepped back, fanning out protectively around us but giving us space.

My mother hugged me so tightly, I feared for my ribs; I hugged her back just as tightly. "We feared the worst," she whispered, refusing to let me go. "Are you all right? Can you fly yet?"

"Yes and no," I answered, trying to keep up with her quick, anxious questions. Though she had been raised avian and was perfectly capable of assuming their poise, my mother was making no attempt to be calm just then. "I'm fine, mostly, but I can't fly. Did any of you see a wolf on your way here?"

"We saw a lot of wolves," my mother answered, stepping back with a puzzled expression. "Kalisa's people?"

"No, a . . ." I sighed. She wouldn't have known Betia from anyone else. "We'll look for her later. What's going on back home?"

"You *are* coming home, right?" my mother asked suddenly.

"Of course. How could you think otherwise?"

She relaxed. "Someone went to great lengths to convince us you left willingly. I can't stay long; there are too many destructive rumors going around in Wyvern's Court. Not to mention your father wanted to go tearing off after you. Nicias can explain everything you need to know. I just had to see you alive and well, and hear from you that you are coming home."

She glanced back at her guards, who were standing at attention. Kel, the sparrow who led the Royal Flight, was quietly conferring with Nicias; he was nodding, listening to her without ever taking all his attention from me. I wondered where Gretchen was.

Nicias excused himself from Kel and crossed toward us. "I apologize for hurrying you two, but Kalisa's runner said that it was lions who kidnapped you." He looked at me for confirmation.

"Yes, the mercenaries who came to Wyvern's Court."

"That being so, I would like to send a few people to track

them as soon as possible." He did not add aloud that he could not do that when all the avian Wyverns were needed to guard me, and the Royal Flight was needed to guard my mother.

My mother nodded, grasping the problem quickly. "Of course. Oliza, we can speak further when you get home; I need to let your father know that you are okay before he goes and does something foolish. *For the gods' sake be careful*," she said imploringly before hugging me again.

"I will be."

"Fly with grace," she bid me before nodding to Kel and shifting back into her hawk form. About half of the remaining guards from the Royal Flight followed her, and the rest stayed with the small number of my Wyverns who were left.

I turned to Nicias then. "Now, tell me what is going on."

"People are frantic," Nicias said, as soon as we had some privacy. "When we found the note—"

"A *note*?"

"In your handwriting," he continued, "explaining that you had left of your own free will. People saw it before the guard did, and half the court was sure— You *didn't* run, right?"

I shook my head, a little dazed. It was the perfect scheme, convincing people that I had left willingly, so that there would be no conflict when Salem and Sive took their respective thrones. But who?

"Who?" I asked aloud.

Nicias shook his head. "We don't know yet. The runner Kalisa sent told me only what they knew—that you had been taken by mercenaries, and that you had been drugged and couldn't fly. Now that we have found you, we *will* find them. Their leader will know who hired them."

"And if Tavisan won't tell you?"

Nicias hesitated, reminding me that some falcons were more than capable of finding the information they desired in someone else's mind.

"I'll bring him back to you," Nicias answered finally. "It will be up to you to decide how we deal with him."

"What else am I going to find when I get home? What happened with Urban?"

"There haven't been any serious injuries since the attack on Urban," Nicias said, "but the marketplace has been volatile enough that I've had to assign a couple of my Wyverns to monitor it during the day." I closed my eyes and concentrated on my breathing. I was a child of peacetime; imagining soldiers policing my home made me sweat. "The three avians who attacked Urban came forward and were arrested. They were all from the Hawk's Keep and had come to Wyvern's Court to visit family during Festival."

"They just confessed?"

"I understand that Prentice put some pressure on the avian community. Your mother dealt with them."

"Severely, I hope."

"Serpiente law would have indentured the three of them to Urban for twice the time that he was unable to work—in this case, until he could dance again—but Urban wanted nothing to do with them. Your mother claimed the time instead and has required them to spend two hours each morning in Wyvern's Court with the scholar Valene, learning about serpiente culture, history, myth and language."

"A fine and cultural tutoring?" I said, incredulous. What could my mother have been thinking? "If they had assaulted an avian, they would have been exiled from the court, possibly grounded. But they can beat a dancer and get away with it?"

"If they had assaulted an avian," Nicias said, "other avians would have been calling for their blood. As it is, your mother feared that exiling them would turn them into martyrs."

Martyrs. What kind of world did I live in, where there were people who would defend three men viciously beating someone? "I want to speak to them when I get back to Wyvern's Court."

"You will have a lot to handle once you are home. Your mother—"

"I *need* to speak to them," I said. "I am sure my mother has addressed the issue to her satisfaction, but I need to look into the eyes of the monsters who would attack a young man just for walking on the 'wrong' side of the court."

Nicias nodded slowly. "Of course." After that, he changed the subject to one that obviously had been gnawing at him the way the attack on Urban had been at me. "Oliza, when you were taken . . . all your guards thought you were sleeping in the nest, and everyone from the nest thought you had gone back to the Rookery. You were abducted from the middle of Wyvern's Court." His voice was raw with guilt. "There were signs of a struggle by the statue in the market, but there were dozens of scuffles that morning and the rest of the day, once word got out about what had happened to Urban. We were so focused on minimizing those fights that it wasn't until midday that anyone even noticed you were missing. And once we found the note, half of your guard—including Gretchen— refused to search for you, saying that if you had left willingly, it wasn't their place to drag you back like a disobedient child. Others hesitated because they wanted to obey our captain.

"Actually, I have charges of mutiny and treason hanging over my head right now for blatantly ignoring Gretchen's orders and convincing others to follow me," he said, "though your parents won't support a trial for either. Unfortunately, by the time I convinced people to look for you, the rain had washed most of the lions' tracks away. We sent out search parties by air and land and found almost nothing. We failed you."

"It sounds," I answered, "more like you were one of the ones who didn't."

Nicias shook his head. "I swore to protect you, Oliza—not the Arami, nor the heir to the Tuuli Thea, but *you*. Even if you *had* left Wyvern's Court willingly, I would still have been bound to protect you. And not to judge you." Reluctantly, he added, "I didn't know whether you had wanted to leave, but I didn't want to lose you either way."

The trip home was long and dismal. Within a couple of days some of the serpents from my guard met up with us, but even then we were short several Wyverns.

These were the only ones who had looked for me, I knew, the ones who would not let me disappear into the night. None hesitated to consider Nicias their leader; apparently he had earned the position. They watched me vigilantly, never leaving me by myself for a moment. I appreciated the security, even though I desperately wanted to walk away from the group a little and call for Betia.

None of the serpents had seen a girl by her description on their way here, and while they had seen wolves, they admitted that they couldn't have recognized Kalisa from Velyo in wolf form.

A few of the serpiente glanced quizzically at the *melos* I wore, but they never asked their questions aloud, so I never had to answer them.

Being surrounded by armed guards made me uneasy. In Wyvern's Court, I had rarely been guarded unless I was somewhere secluded. Never had this many been around me at one time, and never had they been so heavily armed. There had never even been an incident in Wyvern's Court in which my guard had needed to draw a weapon. Ours was not a warriors' society.

Right now, we looked like one. Any stranger who approached us would be seen as a threat, not as a visitor.

Sitting by our campfire and thinking my dark thoughts, I shuddered and felt Nicias put a hand on my shoulder. He sat beside me and stirred the fire in silence.

I needed to tell him the one thing I hated to admit even to myself. He was the only person I knew who might have the power to do something about it. Softly enough, I hoped, that my other guards would not hear, I said, "Nicias, when the lions took me, they . . ." It hurt to face this, as if saying it would make it real. "It wasn't just the drugs that stopped me from coming home sooner. Those wore off days ago. They clipped my wings."

He tried to hide it, but there was a moment when I could see his horror, the very response I was afraid I would get from all my people.

"Is there anything you can do?" I asked. "I don't know much about falcon magic, except for how powerful it can be. There *has* to be a way—"

"I wouldn't even know how to begin," he admitted.

"I know you've been studying further since you came home. I know you have some kind of a teacher. Isn't there someone you can ask?"

"I have been studying," Nicias answered carefully, "but along very different lines. And as much as I hate to admit it, no one on Ahnmik would help me with this."

"Why not?" I demanded.

Nicias averted his gaze, the way an avian guard would when he suspected that his monarch was near to hysterics and he wanted to allow her some dignity. The instinctive, infuriating gesture made something inside me snap.

"Nicias, you are one of my oldest friends, and one of my personal guards. You told me that you preferred not to discuss your time on Ahnmik, and I accepted that, because I trusted that you would tell me anything I needed to know. You brought home Hai, a half-falcon heir to the throne, and I accepted that because I knew that your vows left you no choice but to help a cobra in need. You continue to study falcon magic and continue to tell me little about it or about your falcon tutor, and I have accepted *that* because I trust your loyalty. But now, I ask you a direct question about a relevant, necessary topic, and again you refuse me?"

"Oliza, maybe this isn't the best time for—"

"Nicias Silvermead, I am not asking you as your friend. I am giving you an order, as your princess. What is it that you learned on Ahnmik that pertains to me, that makes you step away from me, that makes you study so hard—and makes you so certain that the falcons who seem perfectly willing to teach you whatever it is you are learning will deny you this?"

"They fear you," he finally answered, looking at me defiantly. He drew a deep breath, trying to get control of himself before he continued, in a softer tone. "You're right. You need to know. Oliza—" He bit his lip, hesitating. "According to the falcon Empress," he told me finally, his gaze distant, as if he hated to say it, "the Cobriana still possess some of the magic of their ancestors—a dormant power that they can no longer use. The Shardae line also carries latent magic, though again, they cannot use it. The falcons believe that, should those avian and serpiente powers combine, they would become active."

He looked at me as I struggled to unwind his nervous words.

"*You* carry that magic, Oliza, but thousands of years have passed since anyone has wielded it, and so it is still sluggish in you. The experience you had with Hai after Urban was hurt—the disorientation and lost time—resembles the episodes many falcons have when their magic first wakes. Often they perform incredible, or devastating, feats of magic they would never be able to replicate. Fortunately, yours was fairly mild, which supports the falcon Empress's belief that even if your magic wakes, it will never be strong or reliable. Probably nothing would have happened at all without Hai's magic acting as a catalyst. But when you have a child, he or she will also be born with avian and serpiente power, and the falcons believe that that child *will* be able to wield it."

I stood and stepped away from him, trying to clear my head. What had happened with Hai and the Obsidian guild had seemed like a fluke, perhaps with a simple and reasonable explanation. I had been raised in Wyvern's Court, not in a falcon's land of magic.

It didn't make sense to me.

"Avians and serpiente are so different," I argued. "They may live together now, but they come from completely different worlds. How could my parents' joining possibly have bred something neither side had in the first place?"

Nicias winced. "Wasn't it the dream of a history where avians and serpiente lived together that led your parents to found Wyvern's Court?"

Only then did it occur to me that Nicias's time on Ahnmik was spent with the only living creatures who could remember the days when the wars between the avians and the serpiente began, who might know *how* they began. "Is it true, then?"

"Not in the way your parents envisioned," he replied. His words seemed carefully chosen. "But both powers, from Kiesha and Alasdair, originated in the same place, two halves of a whole."

There was something he wasn't telling me, and I truly wanted to *shake* him and demand that he stop evading it, but I refused to get sidetracked.

"So my child may have magic," I said, keeping my mind on the future.

"The falcons believe that the power she might have would be dangerous," Nicias explained. "I don't know whether I believe that, but I know that they do. I know that if you have a child and she shows an ability to wield the serpiente magic that you carry, the falcons intend to kill her."

Dear gods. I had ordered him to tell me this, but it made the air seem dense and suffocating. They would kill a child? *My child?*

Nicias caught my hand, drawing my attention back to him. "I may be able to bind the child's magic, or at least control it. I have been working with a falcon named Darien, to try to find a way."

"And when were you planning to tell me all this?" My voice sounded hollow.

"When you chose your mate, so you could discuss it with him. I had hoped that I would be able to give you some assurance of safety by that time."

I couldn't help shivering. "I assume it's occurred to you that if the falcons are so opposed to my rule, they could easily have orchestrated recent events."

"That's true; they could have," he admitted softly. "I can't say that they didn't, even though they assured me they will not interfere yet. On the other hand, if falcons had chosen to remove you . . ." He took a deep breath, his disgust obvious. "Urban wouldn't have been the one who was beaten and nearly killed. You would have been, and it would have been fatal. Further, they would not have gone to great lengths to soften the blow by convincing us that you had left willingly; they would have left us with a serpent or an avian with blood on his hands, to drive us into a civil war."

"You know this of them, and you still trust them?"

"I trust Darien's motivations," he said. "If I didn't, I wouldn't be working with her."

"And despite that, you know that she wouldn't help you with my wings?" The horror of being grounded was something I could wrap my mind around, whereas the atrocity Nicias had just described was beyond my comprehension.

"Darien probably would, but the Empress and her heir would never let her. I had to bargain to keep you safe from *them.* They won't help protect you from anyone else. And if Empress Cjarsa forces Darien to stop working with me, it won't matter if your wings are clipped or not. When your first child is born, if the royal house of Ahnmik does not believe that I can make the child safe, they will kill her, and you, and anyone else who stands in their way."

I tried to calm myself, practicing avian control, wrapping reserve around me like a cold blanket. I couldn't let this information break me.

"We can discuss this in more depth when we need to," I said. "When I declare my king, I will ask you to explain this magic to me: why I have it, why my ancestors had it and why my child will have it. After . . . after I have a child," I said, willing my voice to be level, "we will take precautions, to either control her power or control the falcons if they will hurt her."

The thought made me shudder. We had just ended one war. I was not enough of a fool to try to preserve a child's potential magic at the cost of a war with the falcons. I said, "We will do what we must to persuade them that she is not a threat. Without bloodshed. And as for my wings . . ."

What was losing the sky if I could lose Wyvern's Court entirely?

"I will make do. I need to."

He nodded. "I'm so sorry."

I shook my head.

"Try to get some sleep," he suggested. "We will probably be back at Wyvern's Court by tomorrow evening. Someone there might know something about your wings. But, Oliza?"

"Yes?"

He met my gaze with his very blue eyes, and asked not with a guard's examination but with a friend's regard, "If you don't mind my asking, who gave you the *melos*?"

My hand brushed the soft cloth as I remembered dancing for Betia, and I once again hoped that she was okay.

Softly, Nicias asked, "Have you made your decision already, then?"

I shook my head. "Just a friend," I told him. I was going to have to explain the *melos* to the serpiente when I returned to Wyvern's Court, or risk everyone there jumping to the same conclusion. A female wolf—wouldn't that shock the court?

It was no wonder that, when I slept, the old nightmares invaded my mind.

I was back in Wyvern's Court—and I was armed. I was wearing the blade my mother had given to me; the steel shimmered as if new when I drew it. The instant the blade cleared the sheath, I saw the first wound appear on my own skin. The blade was already bloodied, even though I could find no enemy to slay.

"Oliza, this is madness," someone said, pleading. "There has to be another way—"

I woke with a gasp, shivering even in the warm air, but before I could sit up, someone was beside me; arms were going around me and guiding me back to sleep. For a moment I thought Betia had returned, but I quickly realized that it was just Nicias lying against my back, protective and friendly—the way we had once slept as children in the nest.

I needed that comfort now.

This time I dreamed of the sky as it could only be experienced in flight, something I longed for. I dreamed of the Obsidian guild, and the *melos* I had danced for Betia. I dreamed of running with a wolf, and then of running *as* a wolf.

I half woke once again, wanting to weep at the dreams lost. What wouldn't I give to have those days back?

I turned in Nicias's arms, tucking my head down against his chest, and closed my eyes one more time. I matched my breathing to his, allowing his peaceful sleep to guide me back into the realm.

My dreams were those of an unborn infant, the sound of a heartbeat, and the gentle rhythm of breath indrawn and exhaled.

CHAPTER 17

We returned to Wyvern's Court at midday. For a moment I paused on the hills, watching my people go about their lives, almost as they had every day before. The scene was marred only by the soldiers I could see patrolling the public areas, serpiente on the ground and avians either perched or circling the skies above. A fierce protectiveness swept over me, as well as anger, and fear. This was my world. These were my people. And someone had threatened them.

What do you want from me, Wyvern's Court? I demanded silently. *What can I possibly give to you that will let you be free to live, and love, and dance and sing? Anything you want—except to hurt each other. How can I spare you this pain?*

I jumped when I heard a wolf's howl; I took a step in its direction before I heard a response from another direction, and then another. Just the Vahamil. They used this music to communicate over great distances.

"Oliza?" Nicias asked. I wondered what he had seen in my face.

"Let's go," I answered.

*   *   *

With Nicias beside me, I walked hesitantly into the reception hall in the Rookery, where my mother and father were waiting for me. I knew I was about to face an interrogation.

I had one foot in the door when my father dragged me farther in, lifting me in his arms as if he couldn't believe I was real. My mother followed suit, whispering praise for answered prayers.

I learned from their hasty words that when they had discovered "my" note in my room, Urban had told them of the awkward scene between us in the nest.

"You *didn't* run away?" my father asked finally, his hands on my shoulders as he looked at me intently.

"No," I answered.

"What happened with Urban wasn't—"

"Let's let Oliza talk," my mother suggested, slipping her arm around my father's waist to pull him back and give me room. "What happened, Oliza?"

The answer to that question was trickier than I had imagined it would be. The four of us sat around a small conference table at the back of the hall, and I described as well as I could the attack and what I remembered of my captors, which wasn't much.

"Is anyone tracking them?" my father asked Nicias.

"I've got three of my people on it," he replied. "The lions are a practical group; they won't fight when they know they can't win. That they accepted an assignment to abduct Oliza in the first place shocks me. I didn't expect them to tangle with Wyvern's Court."

Again, Nicias sounded disappointed in himself.

"Continue," my mother said to me.

I described stumbling through the snow, not knowing what it was, sick from the drugs. I told them about Betia saving my life by bringing me to the Frektane. I explained about the poison and for the moment left them to assume that it was why I still could not shapeshift; I wasn't ready to deal with that loss yet. There were more important things to discuss.

I hesitated when I got to the incident with Velyo. Among both avians and serpiente, what Velyo had tried to do to me was a crime punishable by death. Even if my family and the new head of my guard were willing to ignore it—and even that much I doubted—they would not forgive it. It would fracture our peace with the wolves, and in this time of unrest, we could not afford to alienate our allies.

I tried to gloss over the moment, but my mother noticed. "You were in such a hurry to leave that you brought *no one*? I might not agree with Frektane's arrogance, but at least he would have provided you with an escort."

I shook my head, forming my words carefully. "A disagreement arose between Velyo—the new alpha, now—and me regarding a matter I was not willing to compromise on. As an outsider far from home, I was not in a position to question their customs, but neither was I willing to accept them. I thought it best to leave."

My mother sighed, shaking her head. I knew that my explanation sounded like atrocious diplomacy, but I could not defend myself with greater detail.

"Betia walked most of the way with me," I continued. Just saying her name made me feel a little ache in my chest, so I gave as little detail about her as I did about our trek home. "Whenever we heard the lions, we ran," I explained. "So I can't tell you anything more about them from my trip home. Eventually

I ran into Kalisa's tribe, and they sent for the Wyverns. That was when Betia stopped traveling with me."

My story was full of holes. Omitting the Obsidian guild had caused that. I was uncomfortable lying to my parents, so I tried to account for some of the brevity by explaining, "I did receive some other help on my way home, but from a very private group who requested I not discuss them."

Nicias asked, "Are you certain they were not involved with the abduction?"

"I am."

My father said, "I won't insist on knowing why you ran from the wolves; the Frektane are willing to overlook the slight, and I have faith in my daughter's judgment. As for your mystery group, we will trust your instincts there, as well."

"Thank you," I said, before my father added, "As long as you plan to explain where you received the *melos* you are wearing, that is."

"The *melos*," I answered, "was given to me for its earliest traditional reason: as praise for my abilities, and as a request for me to dance. There is no law saying that it must mean more, even though it commonly does. As for the color," I continued, "the giver was a wolf, who doesn't know all the connotations." Among the serpiente, gold represented the bond between mates.

My father nodded slowly, acknowledging the facts but hesitating to outright agree. Even though a request of a dance was the true meaning, for centuries the scarves had been given as courting gifts.

I sighed. "Betia became a very dear friend to me during our time together. She saved my life repeatedly and traveled with me for weeks. I would never have survived without her.

She knew how much I resented the pressure I received from serpiente at home, and how much I wanted to perform."

Both of my parents looked relieved the instant they realized that Betia was a woman, though Nicias was still looking at me with an expression I could not quite place.

What if I *had* fallen in love during my travels? What if I had brought home a white viper from the Obsidian guild? All things considered, bringing that group back into the court would have been an amazing political accomplishment.

Further, what if I had just danced, and some young man I trusted had offered the *melos* with no ulterior motive, as Betia had—simply because he knew what it meant to me? My parents never would have believed me. If they had, they never would have trusted *him*.

There was a short period of silence, which Nicias broke for me. "Would you like to see the note?" he offered.

I nodded. "Please." He handed over the letter, which had been written on the stationery I kept in my room in this very building. "Do we have any idea who wrote it?"

"The best scholars in the Hawk's Keep insist that, as far as they can tell, it *is* your handwriting," Nicias answered. "I don't know of anyone who openly admits to such skill for forgery. Perhaps one of the mercenaries?"

"I don't know. It would probably be helpful in their line of work, but . . ." The letter distracted me, and I began to read.

To rule is easy. To truly protect my people is harder. I write this with tears in my eyes, hoping that perhaps one day my time will come, but believing that for now we are not ready for a wyvern on the throne. We have struggled for twenty years to make Wyvern's Court one land, but one cannot perform such a marriage while both

parties bleed into the dirt and fight against the Fates. Let us heal;
let our children learn peace. And then maybe it will be time.

I leave now of my own free will. This is what I must do. Please
do not seek me.

Oliza Shardae Cobriana

"I don't know who wrote it. I don't know who *would*
write it." I shuddered, standing up.

My parents exchanged an intense glance, the silent com-
munication of a long-married pair. My father looked away
and sighed.

"What?" I asked.

"This is going to be a very delicate time in Wyvern's
Court," my father said. "Your mother and I have been discussing what could be done to calm our people."

"We know how reluctant you are," my mother said, "and
hate to press you for a decision, but we believe that it would
comfort them if you announced your choice for your mate."
She added quickly, "You don't need to go through the ceremony yet or do anything you aren't ready for. Just let our
people know that the decision has been made. People believed too easily that you had abdicated."

My father winced, but he supported my mother. "I know
I was one of those who encouraged you to wait, but perhaps
that was wrong. Technically, your mother and I still rule, but
Wyvern's Court looks to you for guidance. As long as you are
undecided, *it* will be."

I recoiled, refusing to see the sense in their words. "I have
friends and suitors on both sides of the court, but no one I
love, no one I could even *imagine* as . . ."

Protector, companion, friend and lover. An alistair, whom

I could trust with my life and my heart. A mate, whom I could turn to in any moment of joy or grief. A leader, someone to rule beside me. Someone whose *children* I would carry. Someone I would spend my life with, however many more years I had.

"I can't just pick a life partner like plucking a pebble out of a riverbed," I argued. "I know you two made the agreement without love, politically, and found it later—but you were *lucky*, incredibly lucky, and there was no other choice. I don't know a single avian man who wouldn't be horrified to see me stand on the dais and perform a *harja* during the Namir-da—and I certainly don't know one who would dance with me. And I don't know of a serpiente who—"

My mother sighed. "Oliza, I'm sorry. I don't know the answers this time. I only know that indecision can cripple this entire world. And if we can't make Wyvern's Court survive, what does that say?"

I lowered my head. "I'll consider your words," I said softly. Even if I could choose, I remembered what had happened to Urban for daring to steal a kiss. How much would I be endangering any man I claimed to love? "But for now, I need some air. Can we continue this later?"

My mother nodded. "Go. Nicias?"

"I'll be with her," he answered.

"You'll want to speak to your people soon," my father said gently. "They have heard by now that you're back, but they're going to want assurance from you that the rumors of your abdication are false."

"I will speak to them," I promised. *As soon as I know what to say.*

As soon as I knew how to tell my people that I was grounded, flightless. As soon as I could figure out what to do.

Nicias followed me out. I knew he had to, but in that moment, I did not want him near me. I wanted to be alone.

"Oliza, I know why you're panicking," he said, his long legs easily keeping up with mine. "And . . . I noticed that you didn't tell them."

"What could I say?"

"You could say what happened," he replied. "Your mother might know something that would help. More important, she would *want* to know, and you might feel better having told her."

I spun to face him. *Panic*—that was the word he had used, and maybe it was the right one. "Nicias, they want me to choose a mate. I know why they feel I need to, but for the life of me I cannot figure out who to pick. No, not for my life, but for the life of Wyvern's Court. Especially now, with my wings gone. How could I ask an avian man to be my alistair, knowing that he will always see me as some crippled creature whom he must protect and be polite to because he pities her? I *can't* ask a serpiente, not if I'm never going to take to the skies again; the avians would have objected to a serpent before, but how much more will they object if they know I'm not even one of them anymore?"

How can I lead them if I am not one of them?

I jumped when someone spoke behind me. "I'm glad to know you think so little of those who walk the Earth like mortals." The dry, emotionless tone made my skin crawl as I turned to face my cousin. "Don't worry, little queen," she added. "The sky doesn't really matter so much, now, does it?" How many times had Hai been told the same thing since coming to Wyvern's Court with her falcon wings broken and lost? "And at least your serpents can ignore your hawk's blood, if you never show it to them again."

I had felt pity for her before, but this was too much. Nicias must have recognized how nasty the conversation could get, because he quickly said, "Hai, maybe I should speak to Oliza alone."

She shook her head as she obediently moved toward the front door of the Rookery. She paused just before leaving, though, to say offhandedly, "If you had the skill and courage to force-change her, you could heal her wings, my prince. Though in the process Anhamirak's power might ravage your magic as bitterly as it does mine." Nicias's eyes widened in surprise, but before he could respond, she added, "Of course, never having practiced it, you might also kill both of you. And I would find that unfortunate."

Hai turned to me. "Oliza, if you're ever interested in speaking with someone who has a great deal of experience with these magics, a working knowledge of Anhamirak's fire and absolutely nothing to lose from the falcons' wrath or her own self-destruction, you know where to find me. Right now, I'm going to go for a ride. Serpents keep telling me it's just as grand as flying."

She slipped out the doorway while we were both still frozen in shock. In the months since I had met her, Hai had barely even spoken to me, much less said anything intended to be helpful. This was now the second time she had offered to help me in as many meetings.

"Could she really do that?" I asked Nicias.

"I . . . I don't know," he answered. "She *is* powerful, but I didn't think she could control her magic to the extent she is proposing. Maybe I misjudged her there, too." He shook his head. "Her magic is unpredictable, and we've already seen that combining it with yours can have unexpected results.

Just because the falcons don't think your magic is enough of a threat for *them* to worry about doesn't mean that using it can't hurt *you*."

"I know you can't work the type of magic Hai was talking about, but if you were there, would you be able to help control it?"

He paused, thoughtful. "Most of my study the past several months has been devoted to working with Darien to try to control Anhamirak's power, for the binding spell. I can try to help keep Hai's and your powers balanced, but if that doesn't work, I should be able to stop it completely."

We were interrupted by Sive's entrance. Her expression warmed as she saw me. Even Prentice cracked a smile. I tried to do the same, but my thoughts were mired in the argument with my parents, and the strange conversation with Hai; it must have shown on my face, because Sive's expression mellowed before she had even reached me.

"Oliza, I had heard that you had met up with your wyverns and were on your way back, but it is good to see you with my own eyes. Are you all right?"

Not yet, but I hoped I would be. "I don't plan to vacation via mercenary in the future, but I'll be fine. Thank you. And Prentice, I understand that I owe you thanks, as well, regarding the identification of Urban's attackers."

He nodded very slightly. "I was not blind to the fact that my name was on the top of your list. Finding the responsible parties was the only way I could clear my own name, in my queen's eyes, my lady's eyes, and anyone else's."

The response was not exactly what I might have hoped for, but what had I really expected, from Prentice?

"I have spent enough time with the dancers that I could

anticipate how they would react," Sive said. "We hoped that action from the Shardae line would help convince the serpiente that, even with you missing, we had not just forgotten the crime against them."

"Thank you, again. I am glad that both of you were here while I was gone."

CHAPTER 18

After the conversation with Sive, I walked with Nicias along the outskirts of Wyvern's Court toward the dancer's nest. I needed to show my people that I was home, and I wanted to check on Urban.

Nicias had been right to accuse me of panicking after the conversation with my parents. The interlude with Hai and the more rational discussion with Sive and Prentice had calmed me, and now I needed to decide my path.

"The Vahamil are our allies, and though there is obviously a power struggle going on between them and the Frektane, neither pack seems a likely suspect. That leaves someone from Wyvern's Court—I hate thinking of my own people in that light, but I know I must—or the falcons. I know you feel that the falcons aren't behind this, but from what you've said, they seem to have a powerful motive to remove me. Do you really trust them?"

Nicias let out a short laugh. "*Trust?* Absolutely not. The falcons' god Ahnmik might not be *evil*, but he supposedly gave this world manipulation and deceit. If Darien had said she wanted to help me because she felt it was the right thing to do, it would have been a lie. She was in love with your uncle Anjay Cobriana; their child, Hai, is in Wyvern's Court; and Darien hates the Empress and Araceli for supporting the war. She wants to fight them, and that means she will do everything in her power to see you on the throne of Wyvern's Court. Like I said before, the royal house has agreed to give me a chance to protect your child, and I do not think they will go back on that agreement; if they did, I believe they would find a more effective means of doing it. I've been wrong about them before, but if I was in this case, Darien would let me know . . . simply because she is that vindictive."

"What about Hai? She has been here for months now and has rarely spoken to me. When she has, it has usually been incoherent or outright condescending. Now she has offered to help me the last two times I have seen her." The first time had been right before I was abducted. "Hai makes no attempt to hide her loyalty to Empress Cjarsa. Why does she claim to want to help me?"

"I don't know," Nicias admitted, "but she wouldn't do anything she thought would hurt you."

"Why not? I don't believe for a moment that she is loyal to me."

"The only monarchy Hai is loyal to is the one on Ahnmik . . . the one of which I am third in line to the throne." He cringed. "I like to believe that Hai's affection toward me is more than loyalty and magic, but even if it is, I doubt she would hesitate to turn on someone she loved if her Empress wished it. What I *know* is that the only thing that allowed Hai to wake, and allows her to survive in our world, is her tie to me. Betraying you would be betraying me, and it would destroy her."

I needed her help desperately. There was little I could do until I knew whether I had my wings. I had been straddling the line between heir and queen for years. Maybe my parents were right in saying that we had reached a point where my hesitation could hurt my people.

I needed only to decide.

"I know I need to be here," I said to Nicias with a sigh as I thought about the days I had spent in the Obsidian guild. Simpler days, without these hard decisions. "I *am* Arami, and I *am* heir to the Tuuli Thea, and I won't just *forsake* that. But is it so awful that I was tempted? I danced, Nicias, and it was so *pure*. I wasn't queen-to-be. I wasn't competing and being backed into a corner by decisions I am not ready to make. And there was this incredible, perfect moment. . . ."

I thought about the instant after the *hanlah'melos*. It had seemed as if anything was possible. It had felt like . . .

I shook my head.

"I am the leader of Wyvern's Court, and if I have to declare a mate, I *will*." I made this pledge without any idea as to how I would fulfill it. Nicias started to protest, but I cut him off with a motion. "I am terrified that what happened to Urban is just the beginning, that anyone I pick will be in even more danger. But what I've done so far hasn't worked. People believed that I had abdicated—even members of my own guard. The longer I procrastinate, the longer I wait to tie myself to Wyvern's Court, the more speculation and doubt will grow."

"Do you have anyone in mind?" he asked, neither challenging nor agreeing with me. I was grateful for his calm support.

"No," I answered. "Someone known by both groups. A

serpiente who won't be lost without constant company, who won't panic if I ask for a moment of *privacy*. Or an avian willing to learn to dance, and who won't be challenged by . . ." I let out a frustrated cry. "In short, a man who doesn't mind abandoning the culture that raised him, and is submissive enough to let me drag him about. That doesn't exactly sound like a good basis for a loving, equal relationship, does it? And what kind of king could such a man make?"

Nicias shook his head, but before he could say more, he tensed; his hand moved to rest on the knife at his waist as he took a step past me, toward something he had heard that I had not.

A moment later, we glimpsed a flash of white. Nicias unsheathed his blade and moved in front of me.

"If I meant harm, I would not be foolish enough to show myself to a loyal falcon." The voice was familiar to me. I put a hand on Nicias's arm to draw him back as the leader of the Obsidian guild stepped forward.

"*Ciacin-itil.*"

"*Cincarre,* Obsidian," I said. "Nicias, it's all right."

Nicias's expression was doubtful, but he stepped back a little.

"Don't worry, falcon. I do not plan to stay long. I am simply escorting a friend." He looked behind himself and called, "It's all right, dear."

Tentatively, another figure emerged from the woods. My breath left me in a rush when I recognized her.

"Betia."

I pulled her into my arms as gratitude overwhelmed me, washing away the dread in the pit of my stomach. Betia was still in human form; she hadn't gone back to her wolf.

She balked when I tried to draw her into the clearing,

and I spoke quickly. "Betia, this is Nicias; I know I told you about him. He won't hurt you. Nicias—" But Nicias had already relaxed and put his weapon away.

He bowed slightly. "Betia, it's an honor to meet you."

Betia gave a little nod, still watching him warily. However, she let me bring her forward.

"Are you all right?" I asked. "I was so worried about you! I will *never* let anyone hurt you, I swear it. Do you believe me?"

Her gaze flickered from me to the woods, but she nodded again, leaning against me in a way that betrayed her fatigue.

"Oliza," she whispered.

It was the first word I had ever heard her speak, and I spun her about joyfully and then hugged her tightly to myself, not even releasing her when the white viper spoke again.

"She came back to us shortly after you left," he said. "It was obvious that she regretted leaving you, but she did not want to travel alone through wolf territory to find you."

"Thank you," I said. "Thank you so much. Please, if you need anything before you go on your way—"

He shook his head. "I will be fine. You two . . ." He looked past me, at Nicias, as if debating whether to finish, and then concluded, "You should be together."

"Do you want to see Wyvern's Court?" I asked Betia. "Or first, how about a hot meal and a place to sleep?" She smiled, still holding on to me. Her body felt frail; she obviously had not been eating or sleeping well since she had fled from Velyo once again. "I'll take care of you," I promised.

I looked up, intending to thank the white viper once more, but he was already gone. Unsurprised, I turned to Nicias instead.

"For tonight, I'm going to take Betia to Wyvern's Nest. It's public enough that you don't have to worry about my safety, and I don't doubt they'll take her in. Tomorrow I want to speak to the men who attacked Urban, perhaps when they have their meeting with Valene."

"I can come find you shortly before their lesson ends."

"Would you please let Hai know that I would like to speak to her as well, at her earliest convenience?"

"I will let her know."

"Betia, how does an evening in the dancer's nest sound?"

She nodded groggily, already half-asleep in my arms. I scooped her up to carry her, and she leaned her head against my shoulder. She was so terribly light.

Nicias blinked in surprise. "Would you like a hand?"

"You need your arms free in case we run into trouble," I said. "I can carry her."

He shrugged, smiling a little. "I'll speak to Hai. You take care of your friend."

The three of us reached Wyvern's Nest without trauma. Betia found her feet again as we neared the entrance, though she put her hand in mine as Nicias left us and we stepped inside.

We had barely reached the door when we were greeted by a rush of dancers with Salem at the forefront.

"Oliza, thank the gods! I was starting to worry I was going to have to give up this life of hedonism and pick up some real responsibilities." He grinned and hugged me tightly.

"Well, you can relax now. Your future is secure."

He stepped back and regarded me with great seriousness before saying, "First I heard that you had abdicated, then that you had been kidnapped. There were rumors that Prentice— well, they were rumors. There were just as many people up north saying I was responsible, according to Sive. That's the burden of the second heir. But really . . ." His solemn expression cracked into a smile as he gestured at the *melos* at my waist. "If you were going to go off and elope, you really should have warned someone."

"I did not abdicate," I said loudly, so that everyone could hear me. "I did not leave of my own free will, but I have returned safely." I did not mention my inability to shapeshift; I would wait to see whether Hai could work this miracle she had implied was in her power. Because I knew that, like Salem, many of them were more curious about the *melos* than about the state of my health, I added, "And I have not yet taken a mate. The *melos* was given to me by a dear friend of mine, who saved my life more than once these past few weeks." I saw skeptical looks, but most seemed to accept that I was telling the truth, especially when I glanced at Betia to make it clear of whom I was speaking. "Salem, this is Betia. Betia, this is my cousin, Salem."

"Welcome to Wyvern's Nest, Betia," Salem said. "Thank you for bringing our Wyvern home."

She nodded in greeting, a little wide-eyed as she took in her surroundings. Wyvern's Nest was always filled with warmth, movement and music, but right then the air was also thick with preparation for the Namir-da. The holiday was only days away, and there was no force on earth that would stop serpents from celebrating.

Betia jumped as someone else swept in front of us— Urban. Seeing him walking again brought tears to my eyes.

"Oliza, thank the gods," he whispered, hugging me tightly. "When you disappeared, I thought . . . But you're back now. That's what really matters."

"It's good to see you up. How have you been?"

He grimaced. "A little stiff, but the doctor assures me I'll get over it. I still take an escort from the Wyverns whenever I go into the northern hills, even though the crows who attacked me were caught. Avians are being just as careful over here." He looked thoughtful for a moment. "It's odd. There were never a lot of birds around the nest, or out in the market with us in the evening, and we complained about the few who did show up. Now almost all the avians vanish at sunset, and I kind of miss them." He glanced back at someone I couldn't see over the crowd, and added with a half smile, "But then, I seem to have compensated."

"*Oliza?*" At the excited cry, Salem, Urban and the other serpents stepped aside to reveal one of the last people I had expected to see there: Marus. His jaw was darkened by a bruise that couldn't have been more than a day old, and he looked tired, but that wasn't half as shocking as the fact that the big clothes he was wearing had obviously not come from his home. They were serpiente clothes—a *dancer's* clothes— borrowed to cover an avian's more slender frame.

He stared at me with as much shock as I felt looking at him. When he realized he was doing so, he started to try to control the reaction, and then he shook his head as if recalling that members of the nest were made nervous by avian reserve.

"Marus, what are you—"

"Doing here?" he finished for me. "I seem to have moved in."

Urban stepped forward. "I know you two will need to catch up—when you have some privacy—but first, Oliza, Betia, come in, sit down; Betia hasn't even been introduced to anyone. You both look exhausted and hungry. Betia, welcome to Wyvern's Nest. My name is Urban; I'm a friend of Oliza's. This is Marus, another friend. You've met Salem. No one else really matters." A few people objected to the quip, but Urban continued, "Sit down, sit down."

Within moments, half of Wyvern's Nest was sitting or lying somewhere near me, many leaning against me, Betia or Urban. The wolf didn't seem to mind the familiarity. Marus had claimed a spot at the edge of the crowd. The serpents seemed reluctant to sit too close to him. I was still just amazed that he was there.

The time for questions would come later. For now, bread, wine, fruit and meat were passed around and shared by every member of the nest; Betia ate well, and I found that my appetite had also returned.

After the meal, the request was made: "Come, Betia, convince your lover to dance for *us*," someone teased. "It isn't fair at all that we taught her, but she'll only let you see."

My face felt hot. "She's not . . ."

Betia laughed a little, shaking her head. She leaned forward and kissed my cheek as she grabbed my hands and pulled me to my feet. Her brown eyes glittered with a devil-may-care recklessness that warmed me to my toes. If it would make her smile that way, I would dance all night.

The dancers and my mischievous wolf companion all but dragged me onto a low dais at the back of the nest.

I must have danced a half dozen times, performing a few *sakkri* and then moving on to simple one-scarf *melos* dances before, finally, someone called for a *harja*—specifically, Maeve's solo from the *Namir-da*.

"Absolutely not!" I said, laughing. A *melos* could be innocent; a *harja* never was. The *intre'marl* from the *Namir-da* was representative of Maeve's seduction of Leben; the metaphor was not hard to recognize.

There was a sound of disappointment from the audience.

"Someone else perform," I insisted, sliding off the stage near Betia. She swung me about in a fairly good mimic of one of the moves I had performed earlier. "I thought you were *tired*," I pointed out.

She laughed, but the sound was cut off by a yawn that she tried to stifle, turning it into a little squeak.

"That's enough, people; you'll dance your princess to death at this rate," one of the elder dancers said. "Oliza, Betia, everyone else, get some sleep."

There were some grumbles, but people began relaxing, lying down in twos or more. Someone dragged a blanket over Betia and me, and several dancers curled against our backs. I remembered how often a serpiente nest had been compared to a pile of kittens or puppies, and wondered if the wolves ever slept this way. Betia seemed just as comfortable with the crowd as she had alone with me.

CHAPTER 19

Despite having danced myself into exhaustion the previous night, I woke early. Loath to disturb Betia, who was still sleeping deeply, I extracted myself carefully from the pile. Bodies shifted instinctively to compensate for the sudden chill, closing the hole without anyone waking.

I found Urban sitting by the fire, munching on bread and cheese. He offered some to me.

"Morning, Oliza. Beautiful performance last night."

"Thanks."

"I'm sorry about what happened, before," he said hesitantly. "You disappeared, and all I could think was that the last memory I had of you was—" He broke off, then blurted out, "I'm sorry for pressuring you. I didn't realize . . ." He glanced over his shoulder at Betia, and I suddenly understood why he believed I had pulled away.

"Just a friend, Urban. Really," I said.

He raised one eyebrow. "After that little display last night? I've never seen you act that way around a man, Oliza."

I blushed. "I'm royal blood, Urban. I'm in line to the throne. And a royal pair bond has to produce heirs."

Urban cursed, and my mind returned to the argument I'd had with my parents. The dancers would hate any decision that they thought had been made for political reasons instead of love, which meant I couldn't discuss my indecision with any of them—especially Urban. I had walked away from him once, and there would be no undoing that.

My gaze drifted to Betia, who was still sleeping, curled in the arms of a dozen dancers, and from there to a more solitary form.

Urban saw who I was looking at. "Marus approached me the first time I left the nest, a couple of weeks ago. Between his objections to my behavior at Festival and the fight at Salem's coronation, he felt he shared responsibility for what had happened to me, and then for your leaving. He was in bad shape about it and wanted to make amends, so I invited him back to the nest."

"And he moved in?" It seemed a little extreme.

Urban looked down. "He came by a few times. But when I went by his house to meet him one day, his parents forbade him to go with me. They argued, loudly enough that I could hear it from the next room. His mother kept shouting about how it would look, how he would never be considered a suitable alistair by any lady who knew he associated with serpents—dancers, especially—how their friends would be horrified . . . I'd never heard avians raise their voices that way. Marus and I left anyway, and when he went back later that day, they wouldn't let him in. That was about a week ago."

"He's been staying here ever since?" I wondered if talking to Marus's parents would help any or only hurt the situation more. They had both been soldiers during the war and were very conservative, as were many of the avians of their generation.

"Not all of the dancers welcomed him with open arms," Urban said. "I think a lot of them still believe he was one of the avians who attacked me. More of them think he's here just to impress you. But Salem and Rosalind have championed him, and no one has the guts to accuse him of assaulting me when I keep saying I trust him."

I realized that Marus had done exactly what I had told Nicias my mate must; he had crossed Wyvern's Court. He hadn't been accepted by everyone, but here he was anyway, in the dancer's nest.

"Looks like someone was less forgiving," I commented, recalling the bruise on Marus's cheek.

Can I love Marus? I wondered. I looked at my raven suitor and tried to imagine spending every day with him. Tried to imagine someday looking at him the way my parents looked at each other. I knew he was kind, and well-spoken. Perhaps he even had the traits he would need to be a king. But even as I tried to let my imagination run wild, I felt no attraction to him. I had never felt the urge to do any of the crazy things that I had seen my peers do in their attempts to impress the ones they loved.

Such as getting onto a dais with professional dancers of the Obsidian guild, or performing a *melos* in the nest in defiance of all the potential difficulties, and dancing for hours.

Urban grinned, not privy to my thoughts. "One of the others made the mistake of harassing Marus while Salem was around. Salem is such a dancer that sometimes it's easy to forget that he's a cobra, but he has a protective streak a mile wide, and when you trigger it . . . well, he never needed to raise a hand to the other guy. Just stared him down with the kind of Cobriana glare that they say used to make opponents in the battlefield drop dead from terror." He shook his head, still looking amused.

Once Betia was awake, we left the nest so that I could show myself to the rest of my court before my meetings in the Rookery. That early in the morning, the crowd was primarily avian, so our greeting there was much more subdued. The relief in the avian population was apparent in their smiles and in the warmth they allowed into their voices when they welcomed me home, most of them sparing no more than a passing glance for Betia. Wolves in this market were common enough.

Serpiente tended to have late evenings and late mornings, but there had always been a handful who were early risers: a flautist, who had discovered that, though they did not dance, avians did enjoy music; a baker, who sold spice rolls and meat pies; a weaver, famous for his *melos*, who had found a morning niche creating more subdued designs that had since become fashionable as cloaks and shawls in the avian court. That day, there were so few serpiente in the market that I might as well have been in the Hawk's Keep.

Two of my Wyverns, a crow and a sparrow, were taking turns circling above to keep an eye on things. I knew they would keep their attention on me as long as I was in the space they were guarding. Their movements were what drew my attention to Arqueete, the baker, who had drawn her stall off to the very edge of the market.

She smiled tiredly at me. "Oliza, good morning; you are a sight for sore eyes, even though you look as if you've lost a stone of weight since I last saw you. No matter; we'll fatten you up soon enough," she promised. "And is this the wolf I've heard so much about?"

News always traveled fast—none faster than gossip carried by dancers.

"Yes, this is. Betia, this is Arqueete; she has been feeding me every morning I've been home for as long as I can remember."

"Someone needs to; you eat like a bird. Betia, you're staring longingly at one of my pheasant pies. Go ahead and have one; no one else is eating them. Consider it my thanks for finally convincing our Wyvern to dance the *rrasatoth*."

"Where is everyone?" I asked as Betia nibbled at the meat pie Arqueete had shoved into her hands.

She shrugged. "Most of them stopped coming out here right after Urban was attacked—and a good thing it was, since there were dozens of fights over the next couple of days. Then about a week ago Salokin stepped away from his stall for just a minute and came back to find that someone had ruined weeks' worth of work," she said, referring to the weaver. "The rest of the serpiente refused to come out here before noon after that. They all get enough work helping prepare for Namir-da, fortunately."

"And how have you been?"

"Managing," she said. "I refuse to be chased off by a bunch of ruffians causing a ruckus. Sive comes by most mornings and buys breakfast for herself, and speaks highly of me to her associates, so that helps some."

Our conversation was cut short by an avian woman, who cried out with an uncharacteristic display of relief, "Milady Shardae! Finally, you're back. We all feared we might never see you again."

"Princess, how wonderful that you're home," an older

avian gentleman said. "At last, you can put a stop to this madness."

"I am going to—"

"He isn't talking about fights in the marketplace," Arqueete interrupted. "I've been listening to him preach since the day you disappeared. He is convinced that those three birds they arrested are innocent."

"Innocent?" I echoed, staring incredulously at the avian man. "They *confessed*."

"Of course they did!" he said. "With an alistair to the Shardae line accused, what good man *wouldn't* step forward to protect—"

Arqueete offered, "I would believe they confessed to protect Prentice. I would believe he is *guilty*. Everyone knows—"

"It was an absurd accusation," the avian woman who had greeted me a moment before said. Voices were beginning to rise as everyone tried to talk over everyone else. "It is obscene to think that Lady Sive's alistair—"

"Lady Sive's alistair," Arqueete shouted, "would rather lock his mate up in a golden tower than let her have a life."

"Prentice only wants to protect her."

"Protect her from *what*? Salem would never let any harm come to her. He watches her like she's his own—"

"The cobra watches her a little too closely for anyone's comfort."

I imagined that this group had been having this same argument for more than a month; certainly nothing would be settled by my adding to it. I hoped I could lay some of this debate to rest after I spoke to the criminals myself.

I was just about to announce my intentions when Betia stepped deliberately into the middle of the argument. With feigned obliviousness, she nodded thanks to the serpent for her breakfast. I smiled as I realized that she had positioned herself just right: close enough to the serpent to seem friendly, but far enough from the avians to seem polite by their standards.

I took advantage of the moment of peace she had brought to say, "I have plans this morning to speak to the three men who were convicted of the assault. If a mistake was made, I will fix it. If indeed they are guilty, I hope you will trust the judgment of your Tuuli Thea and her heir. Now, if you'll excuse me . . ."

I understood now how my mother could have feared that a serious punishment would turn criminals into martyrs. I heard similar concerns about Urban's attackers as I continued through the market, as well as questions about my own absence. Repeatedly I assured people that the rumors surrounding my disappearance had been exaggerated, that the culprits would be found and that the mercenaries would be taken in for questioning as soon as my guards returned with them. Among the avians, there was no doubt that a group of guards with wings would succeed in finding a group of lions on the ground.

As in the nest, I saw nobody who was afraid, or intimidated or angered by my return—at least not visibly. Avians were better at lying with tone and expression than the serpiente were, but even so, nothing here felt faked.

Betia stayed by my side the whole time, appearing interested in all the goings-on of the market and never wandering off out of boredom as I had the same conversation again and again with my subjects. Just as she had accepted the closeness of the nest, she seemed comfortable among avians.

I thought of her as a forest spirit, a woman from a world completely different from mine, who could flutter among dancers or merchants as if her feet never needed to touch the ground. No matter where we were, she radiated calmness and acceptance.

The wolves had a harder life, yes, but I realized suddenly that they also had a simpler one. They were a people of the seasons, who followed the migratory herds, traded with every culture they encountered and lived at the whims of Fate. The difference between the southern and northern hills of Wyvern's Court, a dissonance that had been the focal strain of my life, was to her as easy to accept as the changing seasons.

I wished that the people of Wyvern's Court could accept each other so easily.

The wolf I liked least stepped through the crowd. I saw him just in time to reach back for Betia's hand.

Velyo's blue eyes widened a little when he saw Betia, and then more when he saw our hands clasped together. Her knuckles were white from gripping my hand so hard, and I could feel her pulse racing where we touched, but she stayed by my side.

"Oliza. *And* Betia," Velyo greeted us, his tone amused. "Well, this explains a lot."

"What do you want?" I asked, trying to keep my voice calm so that we would not attract more attention than we already were. The two avian guards drifted a little closer, keeping an eye on the stranger close to their princess, but they responded to my apparent calm and did not make their presence obvious to Velyo.

"I heard an interesting rumor," Velyo replied, "about you and one of my wolves."

"I would love to discuss rumors with you," I said as I

moved past him, keeping my body between him and Betia, "but I have other obligations."

"You might want to be careful of the company you keep," Velyo warned. I paused, glancing back, even though I knew better. "You're the princess of this land, soon to be queen. You have a reputation to maintain."

"My reputation is neither in trouble nor your concern. Now, if you'll excuse us—" I felt Betia's grip on my hand loosen as she tried to pull away. "Betia, it's all right. He can't hurt you."

Velyo chuckled. "Maybe it would be best, Betia, for you to come back with me, before you cause trouble for your . . . friend."

"She's no trouble," I said, nearly growling. Nearby avians were starting to look concerned, and I struggled to keep my composure.

Before Velyo could make any more snide comments, Nicias dropped to my side and returned to human form. "Oliza, Valene's lesson should be over in a few minutes. You wanted me to come find you."

"Thank you, Nicias."

Perfect timing. Finally I would be able to do something productive. I wanted to put an end to the destructive rumors I had heard that morning. My mother was a wise woman, and I trusted her judgment; I doubted she would have been fooled by a false confession. Also, as much as I disliked Prentice, I knew that he had enough honor never to have let other avians sacrifice themselves to protect him.

"I'll watch out for Betia while you're busy," Velyo said.

I couldn't bring Betia to the meeting; I needed to be the heir to the Tuuli Thea, not just a woman with a friend.

However, I wasn't about to leave Betia with the alpha who had abused her.

"Thank you, but that *won't* be necessary."

"Wyvern," Velyo said, his voice dropping somewhat, "you are aware that you have no authority over my wolves?"

I stepped closer to Velyo, so that my words would be heard only by him. "She. Isn't. Yours. Anymore. Do you hear me?"

"And she's *yours*?" he hissed. "I am trying to look out for you, Wyvern. Even Betia knows she's going to bring you nothing but trouble."

"She *saved my life*," I said. "And she—" She had never done anything to hurt me, and I believed with all my heart that she never would.

I couldn't begin to put into words all that Betia had done for me. How could I explain how it felt to have a friend who didn't care that I was Princess Oliza Shardae Cobriana? How could I describe the way she had given me courage and helped me find the faith and hope I had lost after Urban had been attacked? There was no way to explain how much it meant to me that she had walked into my world and never cringed from it, that she had drawn me up to dance, challenged me, *accepted* me.

"Your face is as easy to read as hers." Velyo sighed. His voice was almost pitying when he said, "You aren't one of my subjects. I don't care what your *preferences* are. But I know what it is to be a leader. You are the monarch of this land; you are your parents' only child. You need a king, Wyvern."

"What does that—"

He put a finger against my lips. "You are not just a woman, and your heart is *not* free to be given away. You need a king, or your parents' bloodline will die. Stop fooling your-self, and *send her away*."

"Oliza?" Nicias touched my arm. "We need to go."

I nodded woodenly.

Stop fooling yourself.

To Betia, Nicias suggested, "If you don't want to be alone in the market, you can wait with Hai and me in the library."

She nodded, her eyes on me. Her resigned expression stayed in my mind as I hurried to my meeting.

CHAPTER 20

I had to put the look in Betia's eyes, and my reaction to Velyo's words, from my mind. I couldn't afford to think about it right then.

My body tight and my face stony, I stepped into the conference room where Urban's attackers were supposed to be. I was going to need every bit of reserve I had to deal with these three calmly.

I had thought that I was prepared, but what I found in the conference room was almost as horrific as the attack itself. One of the "men" waiting for me couldn't have been more than sixteen years old. The oldest—who, I assumed from the similarity of their features, was the boy's brother—was probably near my age, and the third boy a year younger.

I had expected older men, perhaps soldiers—people with memories of war and loved ones lost. These three couldn't ever have seen a battle. Two of them were too young even to have lost a parent or sibling in the war.

These were our vicious assailants?

A few days before, when Nicias had told me what my

mother had sentenced these boys to, I had felt it was too mild. Now, having seen them . . .

I thought about the child who had reached toward Urban at Festival, and how her mother had pulled her away. Who was really to blame here?

I looked at the youngest boy. He was pale, and though his expression was controlled, his fingers were trembling. "What is your name?"

"Shane, milady," he said, in a voice so small I could barely hear it. "Shane Tenahe."

"Brin Tenahe," the eldest said when I looked at him. Unlike his brother, he stood and spoke confidently, as if utterly certain he had done no wrong.

"Luke Redine." The third boy was soft-spoken but shared his friend's poise.

"I heard a rumor, on my way here, that you each confessed out of the nobleness of your innocent hearts. Looking at you, I almost wish it was true—but I don't think it is."

"I did come forward because I heard that Lady Sive's alistair had been questioned," Brin said. *I.* Had he confessed for himself, or for all three of them? "I would never allow my actions to harm the royal house."

"*We* would never," Luke said.

"Would never . . ." I trailed off, thinking of everything that had occurred since Urban had been attacked—all the violence, and guards in the marketplace. "I imagine none of you were alive during the war."

"We've all heard about it," Luke said.

"Have you?" I challenged. "The stories of forest floors so soaked with blood that the trees began to die? The stories of black smoke from the pyres, and the stench of burning bodies so constant that the living stopped even noticing it? The stories of *children* killed, of . . ." So many horrors. "We *have* all heard the stories, but *I* have never been tempted to relive them. You were the first ones in twenty years to pick up a weapon and nearly kill someone who wasn't even your enemy anymore."

I had almost dismissed the younger brother as a child, almost as much a victim as Urban, but he was the one who stepped forward to defend their actions.

"The war never ended," Shane said. His voice wavered a little, but not just from nerves. "Some people say it did, but it didn't. The only thing different now is that people turn a blind eye. We used to live in Wyvern's Court, but we had to move back to the Hawk's Keep because our sister grew old enough to draw serpiente attention and it did not feel safe for us to stay."

"Shane—"

He shook his head when both of the older boys tried to interrupt him. "My pair bond still lives here," he continued. I forced myself to reevaluate my first impression. He was young, but avian boys were raised with an intense emphasis on responsibility and the protection of their families and pair bonds. "I understand that the serpiente have different customs, but why does that give them the right to abuse her? Why does the fact that it is 'their way' mean I cannot take my lady for a moonlight walk without our being propositioned by strangers? Do you know what that is like? I am her alistair, and I am told that I must tolerate her constant *fear*.

"She is fourteen, and she cannot walk through the marketplace alone after dusk unmolested. I fear what would happen to her if she dared step onto the southern hills. There is one small area of this court that is unpolluted by serpiente—the northern hills—and I will be *grounded* before I allow a dancer to skulk about in the shadows there.

"Now, if I have spoken too frankly, if I have offended my lady Shardae—my lady *Cobriana Shardae, Arami*—then I will accept the consequences. I am tired of being silent, and *accepting.*"

Was this the world we had worked so hard to make? This fury had not been bred by war; it had been created in the cradle of Wyvern's Court.

I looked at the older boys.

"I have no pair bond," Luke said, "but I too have family, and friends, and have heard similar complaints."

"Are you telling me that there have been physical assaults by serpiente in Wyvern's Court, and the royal family has not responded?"

"There does not need to be physical violence for people to be harmed," Brin said. "In accordance with our Tuuli Thea's wise sentence, we have been coming here for almost a month now, and we have not ignored everything we have been told. I am aware that most serpiente probably consider their actions casual flirting, that they may have no idea that their 'friendly' jests can ruin reputations, relationships and lives. They don't understand that the pretty girl they just stole a kiss from, such as my brother's pair bond, has possibly never *been* kissed, has never had someone grab her that way and isn't blushing because she is coy but because she is terrified. They're like . . . real birds of prey, snatching mice. Maybe they aren't malicious, maybe they don't mean any harm, but that doesn't help the mice any."

I resisted the impulse to rub my temples. At least I knew they had not confessed falsely.

I considered and threw out a dozen possible responses.

Finally I sighed. "I understand your grievances. I know that Wyvern's Court is still a work in progress. But violence is not the answer."

"We committed a crime," Brin said. "I know that. Violence might not be an answer, but at least it made people recognize that there was a problem."

I took deep a breath and let it out slowly.

"I have another meeting to attend," I said softly. "Gentlemen . . ." Could they be used to help find . . . Their meetings with Valene had to help, somehow . . . or . . . or nothing. I had no ideas. "I'll speak to you again another day."

CHAPTER 21

I drifted from the conference room to the library with my head aching and a heavy feeling in the pit of my stomach. I paused in the doorway to watch Hai, Nicias and Betia for a moment. Nicias looked amused, and Betia was smiling brightly. Hai was wearing her customary detached expression.

Hai noticed me first; she looked up and said, "We were discussing looking into the future."

"You were?"

"And the ethics of looking into someone else's past, or future." She shrugged. "Nicias moralizes like a serpent. Betia listens well, though she doesn't talk much. Or at all."

I wondered what Betia might have said on the subject, or whether there was more wisdom in remaining silent while the two falcons debated.

Betia stood and hugged me in greeting; I leaned against her, desperate for some kind of support. Suddenly a pang went through me. *Stop fooling yourself.*

I've never seen you act that way around a man, Oliza, Urban had said.

The truth was that I had never ever been tempted, just as I had never felt torn about performing the *rrasatoth* dances because there had never been anyone I wanted to perform *for*. Until that day in Obsidian.

I held on to Betia a moment too long, knowing I wouldn't always be able to.

I forced myself to focus on the reason we were there. I had to.

"Hai, I'm sorry for what I said yesterday," I began. "I have never thought less of you just because you can't fly, and I—"

"It would be hard for you to think less of me, cousin, since you think very little of me in the first place," she said offhandedly, as if she found the whole subject silly. "I'm not a falcon to you. I don't deserve that respect in your mind. And I'm not a cobra, either, not kin to you, not in your heart."

She was right. I *didn't* know how to think of her. I found it hard to think of her as family. I acknowledged our shared blood mostly out of a sense of responsibility to her, not out of any genuine affection. The way she drifted into and out of a room, often responding to friendly greetings or questions with an expression that conveyed something close to contempt, had alienated me from the first time we had met.

"I didn't realize you felt that way." Having recognized my mistakes, I wanted to fix them. "I don't know you well, Hai, but—"

"I spoke a *fact* to you, Wyvern," she interrupted, once again snuffing out what might have been some kind of connection before it could be formed. "It was not a plea for compassion. Were I given the choice, I would be in the white city, not here, and I would call Cjarsa my queen, not you. But I do not have a choice. You have come to ask me if I really can fix your wings, or if my offer was just the rambling of a slightly delusional mind. There is no need for this false courtesy before you ask me favors."

"Given how you seem to feel about me, why are you offering to help?"

She lifted her cobra eyes skyward. "My loyalty toward the Empress who raised me implies no hatred for you. I do not care what images of me you hold in your head. I will give you back your wings, if I can, because *I* of all people know what it is like to have the sky, your future, your place in life all torn from you by the shifting tides of Anhamirak's whims. Now, Wyvern, let us see if I can find your golden feathers."

I looked at Nicias, who shrugged, as if to say, *Your decision.* I stepped closer to Hai, and she moved into the starting position of many serpiente dances.

I raised my hands and crossed my forearms, mirroring Hai, the backs of our hands just touching. Nicias stood behind Hai, as if prepared either to catch her or to push her out of the way.

"You really think you can do this?" I asked Hai.

"That, or we could burn down the library."

"Excuse me?"

She gave me an innocent look. "Don't worry. You don't harm Wyvern's Court; your magic isn't that strong."

"Hai, you aren't making any sense."

She leaned back against Nicias, closing her eyes. "You have asked me for my help, and yet still you doubt? Every moment of every day, I touch a thousand different *a'she,* a thousand possible futures. I know that your magic is not strong enough to really burn."

"If you know these things, can you tell me who hired the mercenaries?"

She looked up at me, her eyes like pools of blood. "Now

she asks. But no, I cannot see that. The only way I think I can find your wings is by using your control, that overriding control that will forever keep your magic a whisper instead of the whirlwind it could be. Precious control, which I do not have on my own. Relax, Wyvern. This will hurt."

I was vaguely aware of Betia's warmth behind me when Hai's power first reached me, but then that faint contact, as well as any awareness of the library we were in, burned away.

If this is what her power feels like, no wonder she is mad.

I would have screamed if I could have found my voice, but it was gone, seared away from me. And then I felt Hai, and the power that was at the heart of this agony.

You burn, she whispered in my mind, and in those words I felt longing and envy and fear, all rolled together.

Frozen. When I reached for Hai, her power was like ice. It wrapped around me, seeping deep into my body, contorting muscle and bone.

The magic I had inherited from my parents accepted the falcon's magic like an old companion, and they fit together until I could feel my hawk form again. It had been broken and buried in pain, but now I knew I would be able to grow my wings.

If this could work for one of us . . . could it work for the other? I was not the only one there whose wings had been lost, the only one longing for the sky.

Hai–

No.

I had already reached for her. She recoiled, but it was too late.

My magic had welcomed hers, but hers—

Fractured—

Another power reached forward, something gentler, frightened but soothing: Nicias—

Someone screamed, maybe me. The sound echoed in my head until it became white noise and then hollow silence, stillness.

Like a feather skimming the surface of a sudden draft, I floated into another world.

CHAPTER 22

The world seemed to pause. The air felt heavy and expectant; when I turned, I was hardly surprised to find myself no longer in the library but in the woods. There was a stranger before me. Her eyes widened, and her hand flew to a dagger at her waist—

Suddenly I knew that this had happened before, in some memory I could not quite reach. The instant I became aware of that, I realized that I was not part of this scene. What was happening now was an echo of the past—specifically, the moments I had lost after Hai's magic had interacted with mine for the first time.

Hai's words echoed in my mind: *A sakkri isn't neat like a letter. I was never trained; I can't control it. At least I remember mine. Most without training cannot.*

Sakkri?

Magic. Vision. Sakkri'a'she. *You are about to do something that changes everything.*

My past self held up her hands in a gesture of harmlessness, and the stranger paused, her blade lowering slightly. "You . . ." She looked puzzled, and lost. "This . . . who . . ."

I watched as Oliza-of-the-past spoke softly, facing the confused woman. "You're in the woods near Wyvern's Court," she said. "I am Oliza Shardae Cobriana. Are you a dancer?"

The woman she was facing raised a hand to touch something at her throat: an *Ahnleh*, like the one I wore. *Exactly* like the one I wore. Now I recognized the knife as well; it matched the one my mother had given to me.

"Not a dancer," the not-such-a-stranger sighed.

I understood now, as I had understood then. "The *sakkri*," I gasped, just as my past self had. Once again I was trapped inside the memory. My *sakkri'a'she*, meant to distract my mind and calm me, instead had summoned a vision of my future self.

"*Sakkri'a'she*," whispered the vision.

She wore the *Ahnleh* on a soft leather string. She also wore deerskin boots that went to her thighs, gauntlets of hard leather, and a vest that I now realized was armored.

Her face . . . was mine, but not the one I saw in the mirror every day. The golden eyes were hard, and her expression was painfully controlled. A ragged scar twisted from her left cheekbone, down her jaw, to the edge of her throat—a few more inches, and the wound probably would have killed her.

This was a version of me who had seen war, I had no doubt. The sorrow with which she looked upon Wyvern's Court told me more about her life than I wanted to know.

"They aren't ready," the vision said softly. "There is no answer." She swallowed hard and then explained, "I stayed. I stayed, and when pressured I took a mate. Urban." She smiled a little, but her expression was weak. "He was sweet, gentle, you know. And he was dead within a fortnight, killed at my feet in the marketplace with poison so swift no one saw the source. The riots lasted three days."

She held out her hand, and tentatively my past and future selves touched fingertips.

Vertigo, as time and Fate swirled around us, future and past and present scattering and mixing together.

Suddenly I was on the green marble of the plaza at Wyvern's Court. Sunrise was painting the hills, but I walked through a silent court. Where were the merchants, preparing to sell their wares? Where were the dancers, giving thanks in the mist? Where were the children, laughing, running?

Someone grabbed me, and I went peacefully. This was a dream. Nothing could be hurt here but my heart and faith.

"What do you want, feathered stranger?"

My captor turned me, and I blinked as I saw the leader of the Obsidian guild.

"Dancer, you aren't welcome here," he said bluntly.

Instinctively, I lifted my hand to the *Ahnleh* at my throat, and he smacked it away. "That's the only thing that keeps me from killing you on sight, Oliza Shardae Cobriana." He spat the last two names. "I don't know how you reached our land, but I suggest that you take your wyvern form and fly swiftly and high out of here. Go home to your palace, your forts and—"

Choking back a cry, I violently twisted the world about me, landing on my knees in the same spot but in another reality.

Here, Wyvern's Court was crowded, despite it probably being the middle of the night. There was a festival air that reminded me of Namir-da, and I sighed in relief, trying to shake off the vision of Obsidian.

I should have stayed to ask him what had happened, but I had panicked. I would not do it again.

Leaving the market, I walked up to the dancers' guild, ever the home of gossips. Searching revealed nothing; Wyvern's Nest was gone in this future. Scanning the market from this distance, I realized that there was not a single dais.

I lifted my eyes and saw crows and ravens circling above me, their pattern precise. Guards.

I returned to the market, letting my dream self twist so that I ceased to be Oliza Shardae Cobriana and was instead perceived as a friendly stranger.

"What happened here?" I asked the first passerby I could find. The woman looked at me as if I had lost my mind, and I clarified my question. "I've been away a long time, but when I was here last, there were dancers."

"Oh, well," the woman said, "the dancers all left years ago."

Left implied that they had gone peacefully. "Why?"

"There was a lot of trouble for them," the woman explained. "This wasn't really their place, anyway."

"Wyvern's Court was—"

"Hush, girl, no one uses that name anymore." The avian shook her head. "No, the dancers knew they weren't wanted even before Oliza decided—" She cleared her throat. "Before Oliza decided to do the right thing."

"Which was?" I asked.

"Where have you been, child? Why, she finally picked an alistair. The dancers just got up and left."

Someone behind me spoke up. "Don't let her fool you," the young man said. "The dancers didn't leave. I was part of the crew that took the bodies out of the nest." He swallowed hard. "Someone got it into their heads that Oliza preferred avians, and that they could get away with it. And they did. They say Oliza killed herself, though I don't believe it. I'm more likely to say Prentice killed her."

"Prentice. Sive's alistair?"

"Don't go spreading filthy rumors like that," the woman said.

"Someone killed her," a third person said. "I myself wouldn't accuse the Tuuli Thea's alistair, but someone did it. The wyvern wasn't the sort to take her own life."

I was relieved to hear it. My position in this reality shifted, and I was not surprised to see Sive, sitting in the Rookery's conference hall, a queen upon her throne. Where was the young girl I had known? This woman was beautiful in a cold sort of way, her skin as pale and flawless as alabaster, and her golden eyes fierce.

"Well?" she demanded of the three avians who stood before her, Prentice included.

"Milady, the reports were true," her alistair informed her.

Sive looked away for a moment. "I knew I shouldn't have let her go into those lands, but she had so much faith. And she loved him so much. . . ." She shook her head. "Why didn't I stop her? What kind of promise is *love,* to keep a hawk safe?" she cried out, in a shocking loss of control for a hawk.

"Milady—"

"I'm sorry," Sive said softly. "It has been a very long day. I had prayed that the rumors weren't true. Danica was almost a second mother to me."

My mother.

They were talking about my mother.

What had happened?

"How is my own mother today?" Sive asked. I could see

that she was bracing herself for the answer.

"Nacola is not well, milady," Prentice replied. "The poison—"

Again I pulled myself away, thinking, *Find me a time when there is peace. Please, any god or goddess that exists. Find me a time when I find love, when I take a mate and it does not lead to war.*

Wyvern's Court was gone. No wreckage remained. Instead, the buildings that stood there glittered with what could only be falcon magic.

I shivered.

A small child ran past me, her long chestnut hair trailing behind her. She laughed and turned; her eyes were as golden as my own.

I saw one of the men from the Obsidian guild—the Burmese python I had danced with once—following close at her heels. He picked her up, spun her around and then paused when he saw me.

"Is she yours?" I asked.

"Yes," he answered, warily. "Can I help you?"

"Where is her mother?"

"Ooo." The girl struggled to get down. "I want to chase the butterflies."

He sighed. "Keyi, there are no butterflies."

"But . . ." She started to cry; great big tears trickled down her face. "I want to chase the butterflies."

My eyes widened, and he looked at me with a guarded expression. "Not many people come here," he said. "Did Hai send you?"

"Hai?" I asked, blankly.

He frowned. "You probably shouldn't be here."

"Daddy, let me down!" The girl managed to get free, and she continued running. He hurried to catch up with her and scooped her up in his arms.

"She's a handful, I take it?"

He shook his head. "You really aren't from here, are you?"

"No," I answered.

This time he seemed to look closely at me; he frowned and said, "You seem familiar, but I can't place you." He tensed, holding the girl closer. "You aren't from Ahnmik?"

"The falcons come here often?"

"Look around you," he answered.

"I'm sorry; I have not been here in a very long time. The last time I stood in this spot, Oliza was the heir to the throne."

"No, *I'm* sorry," he answered. "If you are looking for Oliza—" He turned away, his breath hitching.

"Daddy, do you see the rainbow?"

"There is no rainbow, honey."

"Daddy—"

"*There is no rainbow,*" he said, too sharply. Then he fell to his knees, cradling the girl.

Tears stung my eyes. What kind of future was *this*? This was my child; I could feel it. And surely this was the mate I had chosen. But where was everyone else? Where was Wyvern's Court?

What was wrong with the girl?

"Mommy!" the girl shouted, pulling away from her father. She ran to me.

"Not Mommy," her father answered. Looking at me, he said, "I'm sorry, you never told us your name."

"Mommy!" the girl called again. "Mommy, Mommy!"

She was crying now, and I could not help going to my knees and putting my arms around her.

"Please don't encourage her," the man said. "Keyi has a poor grasp on reality. These walls keep her physically safe from her magic, but her mind has never been as safe. Please, Keyi, come here."

"Where is everyone else?" I asked over the girl's head. "The rest of Wyvern's Court?"

He shook his head. "There is no rest of Wyvern's Court. I'm sorry to have to be the one to tell you. We were warned that Keyi would be born with magic. We were warned that it wouldn't be stable. We tried . . . we tried, and Nicias and Darien tried, *everything*, but her magic was too powerful. We had no way to control her and no way to teach her. I know that Oliza wouldn't begrudge her daughter for what she did as an infant, but I think it's probably best that Keyi's mind will never grow beyond what it is."

My breath was coming in ragged gasps. *This* was the world with peace? Was anyone alive?

"What of Sive? Salem?"

He shook his head. "The falcons came."

"Why . . ." My throat closed around sobs when I tried to speak.

"Why am I alive?" he asked. "Because someone needed to care for her, because the falcons wouldn't kill a child. Just lock her in this magical prison, where she chases butterflies and sees phantoms of all the people who once lived on this ground. Hai and Nicias help. So do the rest of Obsidian, as many as Araceli allowed to live. The other serpiente and avian children were taken back to the palace and the Hawk's Keep. I suppose the falcons are raising them."

"Dear sky," I prayed, "is this my future?"

His eyes widened. "Who are you?"

"I'm . . . the past," I answered. For myself more than him, I said, "And I have no daughter. This prison doesn't exist. And Wyvern's Court *does*."

"*Sakkri,*" he whispered. "Oliza?"

I nodded. He stepped toward me, hand outstretched, and then jerked away. "If none of this exists, then I pray you won't let it. *Ever*. Do we even know each other, in your world?"

"We met," I answered. "I was running from mercenaries. We danced together. That's all."

"I remember that day," he sighed. "Better if that is all."

I looked at the daughter I would never have, and held back tears. "When I leave, all this will vanish. She will vanish. And she will never exist."

"And only you will know she could have," he answered.

Gods, why? Why do this to me? If *this* was what the falcons feared, the reason Nicias believed that they would kill my child if she was born with magic, then this was a possibility with any man I might choose as my mate.

"Did she kill me?"

He nodded.

I pulled away from the vision, letting it dissolve, and ended up on my hands and knees, choking on tears.

CHAPTER 23

When the visions faded, Betia's arms were around me and I wept. The wings of my Demi form cascaded down my back; I had wanted them so much, but now they were less important.

I wanted both to remember and to forget everything I had just seen; I wanted never to have known. I understood, then, more than I had ever wanted to. I remembered pulling from the trance after Urban was hurt and struggling to act even as the visions continued to barrage me, slipping me from the present to the past so that I spoke and acted in a haze that I later recalled only in my nightmares.

I struggled now to keep my resolve as the memories frayed like dreams.

"Are you all right, Oliza?" Nicias asked, kneeling next to us.

"Keyi . . ." I tried to hold her face in my mind.

"Hope?" Hai asked, from where she was leaning against the wall. Her skin was flushed, and I could see the sheen of sweat on her brow.

Hope. That was what the name meant in the old language.

But Keyi didn't exist.

"Please, leave me alone for a moment?" I asked of Hai and Nicias. "Thank you for helping. Thank you. But I need time to think."

Nicias nodded and said, "I will be right outside if you need me." With one last concerned look back at me, he escorted Hai out. I was certain that he had not seen the devastating visions I had seen; I did not know if Hai had.

Betia met my gaze questioningly, and I held her more tightly. I did not want to be alone, not truly. And I couldn't send her away, not when she had been gone in every world I had come across.

"Where were you?" I whispered. "Did I chase you away when I became queen, Betia? I must have . . . So much death. Where were you?" I sobbed, looking away. "I had a daughter. And she was mad. And she—"

I could not say it.

Betia lifted my face and brushed the tears from my cheek. Her voice was hoarse from the long months of disuse as she asked, "Were you in love?"

The question, the first sentence she had spoken, made a lump lodge in my throat.

Betia kissed my forehead. "I won't leave you unless you ask me to. I—" Her lips touched mine, chastely. "The future will come. I will be there, if you want me."

She kissed me again, so sweetly that I could not help crying harder. Her lips were warm, her body soft against mine.

"You don't have to speak. Words fade," she whispered. "I know that better than anyone. Words are forgotten; they are regretted. Unnecessary. I know."

So in silence, we held each other until my trembling sub-sided. And when she kissed me once more, I gave in to the temptation, and I kissed her back. With her presence and her touch, she gave me the hope and the warmth that I needed so much.

I don't care what your preferences *are. But I know what it is to be a leader. You are the monarch of this land; you are your parents' only child. You need a king, Wyvern.*

I pulled away from Betia as reality began crashing down around me—as I suddenly remembered why she had not been in the future.

Find me a time when I find love, when I take a mate and it does not lead to war.

I found love. And I took a mate.

They just weren't the same person.

I looked at Betia and saw the hurt in her eyes. "Betia, I can't. . . . We can't be together. Not while I'm queen. Not while—"

A vision of Keyi came to mind, and again the words echoed in my mind:

And a royal pair bond has to produce heirs.

"Oliza?" Nicias had entered the room and was standing beside me.

"Nicias, *please—*"

"Oliza, I'm sorry, but a group of our guards just brought the mercenaries in."

The lions. I needed to talk to them. Needed . . .

I want to chase the butterflies.

Again, I struggled to keep the dream in focus. But I also wanted more than anything to forget it, to curl in Betia's arms and pretend that the future was easy.

"I need to talk to the mercenaries," I said.

Betia nodded, her expression resigned. I couldn't help it; I kissed her again, tasting her lips and drawing strength from her embrace for what I needed to do. I didn't care what Nicias thought.

"The lions hunted sometimes with us," Betia said. "They only do their jobs. Don't hurt them?"

I smiled, moved by her protectiveness. The lions had no formal kingdom and had always been at the mercy of the laws of the lands that they visited. The punishment for treason was severe in both courts, but in this case I could promise. "I won't hurt them." Needing her support, I asked, "Would you come with me to speak to them?"

Betia hesitated, but then she gripped my hand and helped me stand.

CHAPTER 24

Tavisan and nine of his people were waiting in the Rookery courtyard, surrounded by my Wyverns and additional members of the serpiente and avian guards. It was the place where I had first met him; it was also the place where I had woken up after the unintended sakkri.

"Let me through," I told my guards as they tried to keep me from getting too close to the lions' leader. Too many people were there. "Nicias, I want to speak to Tavisan alone."

"Oliza—"

"*Now.*"

His eyes widened at the command, but nevertheless, he escorted Tavisan from the mass of soldiers to the far edge of the Rookery, where, if we kept our voices down, we would not be overheard. Betia hesitated and then, at my gesture, followed us.

"Betia Frektane, an honor as always. Oliza Shardae Cobriana, I hope you take no offense if I say I had not hoped to see you again." His voice was soft, and his body seemed tired.

Nicias had given us some room, but he didn't move so far back that he could not intercede if Tavisan tried anything.

I didn't have time to argue with him. Voices were echoing in my head, and I grasped at them, needing to remember. . . .

The dancers didn't leave. I was part of the crew that took the bodies out of the nest. . . .

Tavisan took a deep breath. "I know what you are about to ask, milady, but I cannot tell you the name of my employer. I was instructed not to tell anyone, my own people included, unless my refusal to speak put me in danger."

"You don't think you're in danger here?" Nicias demanded. "You abducted our queen. For a reason I do not comprehend, she is willing to show you lenience. I think it would be in your best interest to answer her."

Tavisan, I need your help.

Milady, what is wrong?

I finally understood the argument that had echoed in my mind frequently since Hai's magic had first triggered mine and I had spun the *sakkri'a'she.*

Oliza, this is madness. There has to be another way.

Almost two months before, I had woken from these visions the same way I had this time, desperate to protect the future from the horrors I had seen. I had gone to the only person I knew who might be able to help me do what Hai had warned me I would: *change everything.*

There was no time to be subtle. "I hired you."

"What?" Nicias asked in shock, but I ignored him. No time.

"I know it's the truth. I remember now." More important, I remembered *why.* I couldn't let the horrors I had seen become reality, and there was one thing they had all had in common.

The one thing I had begged Tavisan to help me remove.

Tavisan hesitated but then nodded. "You told me that you needed to leave Wyvern's Court, but that you feared you would soon lose the knowledge of why. You were the one who ordered me to strip your winged forms, so that you would not be able to return easily." His gaze dropped. "We did not anticipate that the Frektane, whom we have worked with before, would be a problem."

I want to chase the butterflies. . . .

"Nicias . . . release them, all of them. I need to go."

I want to chase the butterflies.

I grasped at the memory but couldn't quite find it. Why did those words bring an ache to my chest?

I want to chase the butterflies.

I kissed Betia's cheek and whispered, "I will meet you . . . in the nest. There is something I must do now. I love you."

I needed speed; I needed my wings. I shifted into my wyvern form, nearly shrieking with the relief of finally unfurling my wings again. I would have loved to take to the skies and soar, but in that moment, I had other things to do. I whipped out the doorway, past Nicias, who I knew would follow me as soon as he had changed into his own form for flight.

Sive let out a little gasp as I landed inches in front of her, finding my human form again; I had stopped and shifted so swiftly that she had to grab my arm to steady me. She was alone, luckily. I did not want Prentice as an audience just yet.

I swallowed thickly. Could I really do this?

I asked, "Could you do it, Sive? I've heard how highly your people speak of you, and I know that you would treat them well; you think swiftly and are as polished as any hawk ever was. Could you rule if you had to?"

She froze. "Oliza, are you all right?"

"Never mind me," I answered. I couldn't think about myself right then.

I couldn't think about how I had always expected to one day be their queen. All my life I had considered Wyvern's Court mine.

Mine to protect, before anything else.

"Both of our mothers are still alive; you would not need to take a throne immediately or even soon. I assume you would inherit it when an avian queen traditionally does, when you have your own child, years from now.

"Would you do it?"

She nodded slowly. "If I had to, Oliza. But you are the wyvern of Wyvern's Court. I could never replace you."

"I'm not asking you to replace me."

I found Salem in the market. This time I landed a little ways back. The cobra was engaged in lively banter with a pair of merchants, both of whom were looking rueful but honored by his presence.

He stepped back from them with a self-satisfied nod and quickly noticed me.

"Good morning, cousin." The lighthearted sparkle in his eyes almost made me forget my purpose, almost made me remember simpler times.

The burden I was about to put on him . . .

"What would you have done if I had never returned to Wyvern's Court?"

He frowned. "You don't think I believed that nonsense about your abdicating, do you?"

"No, I don't," I said. "I'm just asking what if. If I was gone, what would you do?"

Slowly, now visibly worried, he answered, "I'm no wyvern."

"I'm not asking you to be," I said. "Could you be Arami for the serpiente? Lead this generation, in peace, so that maybe in the future . . ." My voice was wavering.

Salem began to pace, his garnet eyes flashing. "Oliza, you will be a good queen. *No one* cares more about Wyvern's Court than you do, and—"

"If I rule them, it will *destroy* them," I said. "I would be their queen if they would allow me, if Fate would allow me, but my first duty as their leader is to keep them safe. Could you do it?"

He sighed heavily, running his hands through his hair. "They like me, Oliza, if that's what you're asking. If anything ever happened to you, they would accept me as Arami, as Diente. But, Oliza—"

I didn't wait for him to protest any more. I returned once again to Wyvern's Nest. I kissed the doorway, knowing that I would probably rarely see it in the future. I could not be in Wyvern's Court without usurping power from Sive and Salem. I wouldn't be able to stand it.

There could be no indecision.

I was trembling as I walked into the nest, because I knew that I could not change my decision, no matter what answer

I received there. I could not keep Wyvern's Court or my place as its princess; I could not keep any of the things I had assumed would always be mine. I could only pray that there was something—*someone*—I loved that Fate would not rip from me.

Betia greeted me hesitantly. I caught her hands and pulled her to me. I sensed her concern and support for me, and they calmed my nerves as I kissed her. I remembered those simple words she had spoken, when she had promised never to leave unless I asked her to.

And then I went down on one knee.

"I don't know what kind of life we might have together," I said, never looking away from her warm brown eyes. "But I know I would protect you with the last scrap of my soul. I know I want to *be* there for you, to hold you, to dance for you, to hunt with you, to be with you no matter where Fate takes us, because it's the sound of your heartbeat that comforts me when I drift off to sleep, and I know I—I cannot offer you royalty. I'm not sure what I *can* offer you—but myself. Hopefully that is enough, because I love you, Betia, and I do implore you to be my mate."

Tears gathered in her eyes, and my stomach twisted and my heart pounded in panic. I had to give up Wyvern's Court. The decision was made and set in stone, no matter what happened.

She knelt in front of me and squeezed my hand gently.

"Wolves mate for life," she said softly.

I smiled and said, "So do wyverns."

"I love you," she whispered. "I . . ." She shook her head and said again, "Words fade so easily."

Her lips touched mine, and she held me as if she would never let go—not even when her fingers found the feathers at my nape, or the sparks of red and gold in my hair. She had not pulled away from me in the closeness of the nest or objected to the calmness of the avian market; she knew every side of me, had listened to all my dreams and had never rejected any part of me.

She didn't have to say the words aloud.

Someone behind us whistled, which made us both recall at the same time that the nest was rarely empty. Even though I had paid it no mind when I had entered, there was a crowd watching us.

Betia laughed.

"I'm going to need to talk to them," I said apologetically.

She nodded, not quite giving me up yet; she slid her hands down my arms to twine her fingers with mine again.

"Betia, you're the one who has been with me this entire time. You know what I'm about to do?"

She nodded. "Speak to your people. I will wait for you."

Suddenly panicking again, I gripped her hands. "Am I doing the right thing? It kills me to give them up, but I really think this is the only way. I know what people will say. They'll accuse me of being afraid. Am I just a selfish coward giving up because it's getting hard?"

"Selfish coward?" she repeated with some confusion. "From the time I met you, you have spoken of Wyvern's Court with love, and pride, and a sense of home that I envy. You have spoken of yourself as belonging to them. Wyvern's Court is your world. It is *you*. It . . ." She shook her head. "Words, words. I just know that it can't be selfish or cowardly to give up everything you ever thought you were, in order to protect them."

We kissed again, quickly, and then looked up at the dancers, who had backed off enough to give us some privacy.

Urban took my glance as an invitation to step forward. His limp was a dagger to my heart, but it reinforced my determination.

"I'm sorry" was the first thing he said. Only then did I realize that much of the nest must have seen the pained look on my face in addition to the interlude with Betia. "I know we teased you two a little, but I don't think anyone really thought—" He looked stricken as his gaze fell to Betia, and I realized he was apologizing to *her*. Turning back to me, he said, "I take it this means you've made your decision?" I struggled to come up with an answer as he shook his head and said gently, "I can recognize a goodbye when I see one, Wyvern."

He thought I was saying goodbye to Betia and preparing to declare a mate. That was what the apology was for— Wyvern's Court's taking me from her. If only he knew how much I was really saying goodbye to.

"Would you help gather the serpiente in the market?" I asked him. "I need to make an announcement."

He nodded. "I'll tell the others. And I'll bring Marus."

"Thank you." I separated grudgingly from Betia. "I'll meet you there?"

She nodded, and again I found my wyvern form. I stopped briefly to inform Nicias that I needed to address my people, and I asked him to gather the avians.

Then I sought my parents. A courier, whose eyes were wide as he beheld my rumpled hair and harried expression, hurried to fetch them once I reached the Rookery.

"Oliza?" My mother sounded worried as she and my father came into the room.

My father took one glance at me and then poorly suppressed a smile as he came to the obvious conclusion. He cleared his throat.

"I've made my decision," I told them. "I need to address our people. I'd like to do so from the market, unless you have another idea."

My parents looked at each other.

"Do we get to know the outcome, or shall we also wait?" my father asked, his smile suddenly a little more strained.

I hesitated. I wanted to tell them but was worried that they would try to talk me out of my decision. The images from the *sakkri* had already faded to a point where the strongest thing I remembered was the sense of absolute desperation. I remembered what I had thought of them, remembered that I had seen the devastation caused by every choice I made, but the specifics . . . the faces . . . they were disappearing.

I was happy to lose the details; they had hurt too much. I was also happy that, unlike last time, I was not losing time—perhaps because Nicias had been there to balance the vision and cut it off cleanly at the end.

"I will speak to you along with our people as soon as they have gathered—which, hopefully, they are already doing. If you're willing to wait."

They both looked worried now. I remembered the stories I had heard of the last such "announcement," when my parents had told their respective people of their choices: to get married and unite the avians and the serpiente. Many people had been horrified.

But in the end, the war had stopped.

"We can wait," my mother said, and I knew that it had taken all her avian poise to say that. She grasped my father's hand. "As long as you are certain."

"I am."

CHAPTER 25

Within the hour, I stood on a dais at the center of the market, near the glittering wyvern statue. I took a deep breath, seeking strength.

My eyes fell to the small group immediately in front of me: my parents; my mother's mother; Salem; Rosalind; Sive; Prentice; Nicias; his parents, Andreios and Kel; and of course, Betia.

Hai was conspicuously absent.

You are about to do something that changes everything. Her words had begun all this, and now I wondered if she had known that it would lead to this moment. What had she wanted?

Had she spoken as a cobra, protecting Wyvern's Court, or as a falcon?

What I needed to do remained the same either way.

Behind my family and all around the dais was a seething mass of curious avians and serpiente, who had all hushed the instant I had landed and taken human form.

In the sudden silence, I could feel my heart pounding and hear my blood rushing.

"Twenty-one years." I sighed and then cleared my throat before beginning again. "Twenty-one years ago, in the *sha'Mehay* dancer's nest, the dream that would become Wyvern's Court began." My voice carried this time, ringing through the market. "The dream was inspired by a symbol, and by the word *alistair:* protector. It spoke of a beautiful world, a peaceful world—one in which serpiente and avians lived side by side long ago. More important, it spoke of another world in which they would do so again.

"I look into this crowd today and see vipers and sparrows, taipans and crows, and all these faces prove how far we have come." At that moment I saw Marus at the periphery of the crowd. He was staring longingly at his parents, who were standing farther off. "Simultaneously, they prove how much further we still have to go."

My people were watching me, their faces curious and excited. I knew that what I was about to say would change those expressions.

"I've been a fool."

Those who had been silent and attentive began to shift and grumble as they sensed that this announcement was not about to go the way they had expected.

"We dreamed of a world in which these two kingdoms would become one. But that's all it was—a *dream,* ruled by the logic of dreams.

"I love the southern hills of Wyvern's Court. I love their dance. I love their laughter, their comfort, their expression. I love their passion." I continued with just as much sincerity, "And I love the northern hills. I love the rhythm of the skies. I love the debates, the music. I love the *simplicity,* and the beauty of shy romance.

"I love this entire world.

"I love these *two worlds*.

"And that is what they are.

"Nearly two months ago, a young man, a dear friend of mine, was severely beaten for daring to cross the market from his world to the northern hills. More recently, another friend lost his home, his family, for trying to do the same.

"Every day in the market reveals the segregation and the prejudice that we have almost come to take for granted. We say, 'That's their way, not ours,' and we walk away ignorant. Or worse, we say, 'Well, at least we aren't at war,' when we are *killing* each other with fear and hatred. We ignore the slander because at least it isn't blades. We ignore the pain because, thank the sky, it isn't blood."

I fought the urge to pace on my dais. People in the crowd were averting their gazes as they recalled their own actions. Only Nicias kept his eyes on me.

Marus's parents noticed him in that moment. But when Marus took a step forward, his mother turned her back on him.

"I am of you, of all of you, avian and serpiente. I have for all my life wondered how, beyond my very *existence*, I can prove to you that we can live together. In my parents' time, the mission was to stop the bloodshed, but in mine, my goal has always been to stop the *hatred*.

"And I have never known how."

I paused to gather my thoughts, drawing air into my lungs, which felt constricted. Betia smiled up at me, her eyes holding absolute trust.

"These two worlds are different, so different that I do not know if they can ever be made one. I cannot say that one set of values is superior. I cannot say that a child should be raised one way or another. I cannot destroy one culture to assure that there is no strife.

"I should not. And I *will* not.

"So all I can do is give you to yourselves and let you live side by side, each generation trusting a little more."

I saw confusion in my people. My mother was gripping my father's hand so tightly that her knuckles were white.

"I would be your queen if you would allow me. I would be honored to lead you. But now, I do what I must."

What do you want from me? I had demanded of them once. I had prayed to the Fates for guidance, time and again, screaming to them, *How can I give peace when they do not want it?*

"My generation has tasted peace, and I have faith that they will safeguard it. And I have faith that someday, when the past is further behind us and fear and hatred have been supplemented by understanding, the time will come when a wyvern can grace your palace.

"But that hour is not now." It was time to change everything. "We have tried to marry two worlds, but one cannot perform a marriage while both parties hold knives to each other's throats. One cannot sew two pieces of cloth together while both unravel. Let us heal. Let the land know peace."

I stared at the faces around me, and I announced, "As of this moment, I formally renounce my claim to both thrones, avian and serpiente."

I tried to avoid looking at my mother, but I could still see her sway, then lean against my father's tense form.

"I name Irene Cobriana's son, Salem, Arami, next to be Diente of the serpiente."

I held out my hand to the cobra, and he stepped onto the dais, face composed so that his people would not be troubled.

I knew that he would have liked to argue with me, to shout and rail against my decision. He hid his emotions from the rest of his people, comforting them, his first sacrifice of *self* for the throne he had never expected to hold.

It would not be the last. This title I gave him was no gift.

He said softly, for my ears alone, "They need you, Oliza."

I shook my head, but like him, I could not let our people see me breaking inside. "I've given them what I can. It's up to you now." Turning to the crowd, I continued, "And Sive Shardae, my mother's sister, shall rise as Tuuli Thea of the avians."

She nodded as Salem helped her onto the dais. She was as externally composed as we were—as if we had planned this months before, and neither dissented. We needed to be in agreement in front of our people. They both knew that.

"I share blood with both of them," I concluded. "I am living proof that we can live without hatred. So I give you to yourselves and ask that you remember, and you teach your children, and they teach their children. Learn, trust, just . . ."

I would have given them everything: all of me, all I had and all I was. Instead, all I could give them was my faith and desperate hope that they would—

"Just *try*. The future, my people . . . the future is all we have."

I stepped down from the dais, leaving Salem and Sive to address our—*their* people. My mother and father instantly came to my side.

Both looked as if they wanted to speak, but neither did at first.

"It was the only choice," I said.

My mother swallowed hard. "Oliza, I know how hard leadership can be, and how impossible the future seems sometimes, but—"

"*Staying* would have been easier; it's leaving them that will break my heart. But it would have been selfish to keep them. I can't give them what they need. Please, trust me." I drew a breath and added, "And even if you can't . . . Our people are going to be scared. I know that. They need to see that you believe in them. Sive and Salem are going to need your support. So, please, don't fight me. It's done."

"But what are you going to do?" my mother asked. There were tears in her eyes.

"I'm going to leave for a while, so Sive and Salem can show Wyvern's Court that it can survive and prosper without me. I'll be with friends." I thought of the Obsidian guild as I said it. They would take me in. "And I'll be with my mate."

Betia had pushed through the crowd to reach me as my parents and I spoke, and now she took my hand. My mother closed her eyes a moment, speechless.

Finally my father sighed. "Oliza, this isn't necessary. If you aren't ready, then—"

I winced and said, "If you are referring to my leaving, it *is* necessary. I know that you may never understand it, but please, *trust* me. I am the daughter you raised, and I am doing what I must for the sake of our people." He started to argue, but I continued, "And if you are referring to Betia, you should be careful. I know you are upset, and shocked, but I love her. I won't have you treat her like she's some kind of excuse."

My mother broke out of her paralysis. "That isn't what we . . . who we . . . Oliza, are you *certain*?"

"More certain than I have ever been about anything."

She started to speak again but then hugged me instead. She looked at Betia and said to me, "We love you, Oliza. And we trust you. We just— Good luck."

My father nodded and seemed resigned when he said, "Treat her well, wolf."

Betia and I walked through the market toward the edge of town in silence. I was barely aware of Salem, who spoke behind me to a crowd that was growing more and more restless, or of my people as they moved aside to let me pass. Some of them called my name, but I had to shake my head and keep walking. I saw several of my Wyverns—mine no longer, but performing one last duty—lining up to try to hold back the avians and serpents who were trying to follow me.

Suddenly Marus and Urban stood before me, side by side, as if they had planned this final vision of the world of which we had all once dreamed.

Marus started to speak, stopped and then drew a deep breath as if to compose himself. Urban said, "Oliza, I know we aren't perfect, but . . . don't give up on us. We can still—"

I touched his face, silencing him before he made me cry. "I have all the faith in the world in you, both of you, *all* of you. If I was needed, I would never leave. If ever I *am* needed, I won't be far. I'm not abandoning you. Just . . . letting you spread your wings."

Urban smiled wryly. "But I don't have wings."

"I do," Marus offered, voice slightly choked. He gave up on the idea of reserve and hugged me. "We'll make you proud," he whispered. "Take care of yourself."

Then it was Urban's turn. He kissed me on the cheek and smiled at Betia. "Take care of her, Betia. She's precious to us."

There was one last person I needed to speak to. Nicias caught up with us just before the woods' edge.

For a moment, we regarded each other in silence.

"I understand," he said at last, quietly. "I hate it, but I understand."

"You may be the only person in Wyvern's Court who really does."

"People are going to be angry. Hurt."

"I know. I wish it wasn't so, but . . ."

"There's no other way," he finished for me. "I don't know all of what you've seen, but I've seen enough myself to understand. We'll manage; don't worry about us." He added, "And I'll feel better knowing that you and your mate are taking care of each other."

Tucked against Betia's side, I said, "Thank you for that, too. My parents were a little shocked."

"Your parents," Nicias said, "haven't heard the way you've talked about her. They haven't seen the way you look at her. I think I knew before you did."

"She *was* a little slow," Betia said, teasing. I started to defend myself—and then just kissed her instead. She was right.

Betia led once we were in the woods. I knew she would find our destination without difficulty. This was, after all, her realm of expertise.

I was not surprised when Velyo intercepted us. With an arrogant smirk, he said, "I listened to your little speech—quite heartwarming. It's nice to see that you can justify walking away from them to be with your fling."

I went rigid.

This time, Betia came to *my* defense. "He will never understand," she said. "He doesn't know what it means to sacrifice to protect your people."

Velyo's eyes were blue flames as he turned on her, clearly

as furious as if she had struck him. "Do not speak to me about leadership. You turned down my offer when I would have made you queen of the Frektane. Is this what it takes to win your hand? A queen abandoning her throne? I should have had the pack hunt you down, before—"

My fist met his jaw, hard enough to send him stumbling backward.

"Don't you *ever* threaten her," I snarled. "In fact, I think it would be best if you just left us alone."

He regained his balance, his hand going to his face.

"Abdication means I'm free to make my own choices, for myself," I pointed out. "It means my word isn't that of my courts. It's simply mine. Tempt me, and I'll dance this dance with you."

"So you're proposing what—to kill me?" Velyo asked. "You won your place as princess by birth, Wyvern, and you weren't strong enough to hold it. I won my right to rule through blood and my own strength. You have no chance of winning, but you want to try to challenge me for one of my own people?"

Fury rippled through me, and I leaned toward him. With my lips only an inch from his throat, I whispered, "You should know, Velyo, that a cobra's bite while you sleep will kill you before you can wake."

He jumped back from me, and I smiled, betraying a cobra's fangs. My eyes, normally a hawk's gold, had become a sea of blood marked only with slit pupils.

He was caught in my gaze like a baby bird. Like prey.

I added, "And Velyo? Everyone sleeps sometimes."

Betia growled, on the verge of shifting into a more deadly form. Velyo looked back and forth between us, not quite managing to hide his fear.

Finally he stepped back.

"She's yours, Wyvern. Seems you two deserve each other." He shifted shape and loped away in his wolf form, with his fur bristling and his tail down.

I turned to Betia and pulled her into my arms. "Thank you," I whispered.

But Velyo's words still bothered me. How many people thought that I had abandoned all of Wyvern's Court just to follow my heart? It was a beautiful, romantic idea, but leadership left no such luxury. How could Betia respect me, respect *us*, if she thought—

She shook her head. "I would have said no."

"What?"

"If you had wanted me despite what you needed to do," she said, "I would have said no. I am too Frektane"—she grimaced a little as she said it—"to love someone who would betray her duty. You are too Shardae Cobriana to love someone who would ask you to. And I love you. So ignore Velyo."

Wise words, very wise words.

We returned to the Obsidian guild, who took us in as friends and dancers without asking questions that I suspected they would quickly learn the answers to anyway. In the abandon of the evening, I performed blade dances and *melos;* after a long, lingering look at my mate, I performed the sensual *harja* for the first time. I danced *sakkri* of thanks and love and passion and freedom.

Betia shared myths and stories from her people and taught us songs she said were often sung on the cold nights. Her voice was a husky alto and blended with mine very well. When pressed, I shared some of the songs and stories of my mother's people, which the Obsidian guild had never heard.

197

As the dawn neared, I curled against my mate's side, listening to her heartbeat and enjoying her warmth. Sleepily we murmured of the future to each other.

I did not know what the next days would hold, for me or for my world. The next night would be Namir-da, and the serpents would dance as they always had and they always would. Avian parents would whisper to each other about scandal in the knowing way that elders had; meanwhile, their children would sneak out to watch the rituals with wide eyes and fascinated minds.

I had to trust Salem, Sive and my parents to take care of Wyvern's Court. I had to trust Wyvern's Court to let them. I had not left them an easy path, but at least now they had one.

Toth'savirnak
Savirnak'toth
Sacrifice of love, sacrifice for love.
Fate is gentle and harsh; she gives and she takes.
A'le-Ahnleh

About the Author

Amelia Atwater-Rhodes grew up in Concord, Massachusetts. Born in 1984, she wrote her first novel, *In the Forests of the Night*, praised as "remarkable" (*Voice of Youth Advocates*) and "mature and polished" (*Booklist*), when she was thirteen. She has since published *Demon in My View*, *Shattered Mirror*, and *Midnight Predator*, all ALA Quick Picks for Young Adults; *Hawksong*, a *School Library Journal* Best Book of the Year and a *Voice of Youth Advocates* Best Science Fiction, Fantasy, and Horror selection; *Snakecharm*; and *Falcondance*.